The taste

Abby glanced at herself in the bathroom mirror and literally did not recognize the face reflected there. Large hazel eyes were made more prominent by too much mascara, short tousled hair, cheeks blushing scarlet, mouth swollen and reddened from the heated pressure of Durango's kiss.

A sex goddess.

A passionate *überbabe*.

So this was what it felt like...a bold vixen, a passion hound, a wicked femme fatale. She was now the kind of woman men bought naughty outfits and sinful chocolates for. Tonight she wouldn't worry about what the neighbors might think. Tonight she was a rowdy sex nymph ready, willing and eager to take a big juicy bite out of life.

Emboldened, Abby stepped out into the hallway and headed for the club's dance floor. But Durango captured her from behind and began to pull her into a long, slow, moist, deep kiss.

Hadn't she read somewhere about a connection between how a man kissed and the way he performed in the bedroom?

Abby's heart fluttered. If that was true, she was in for one hell of a fine treat.

Dear Reader,

Last spring my husband and I visited Sedona, Arizona. I was awed by the red rock formations and struck by the incredible energy field surrounding the place. The Native Americans there consider it sacred ground.

There are numerous energy vortexes in those compelling mesas, and if you're attuned you can actually "feel" the vibrations coursing up from the earth. My mind started swirling. Just imagine making love where the energy field emanates not just from you and your man but also from the strumming force of the earth.

All your senses are intensified and stronger, and they resonate. You're a tuning fork at perfect pitch vibrating with your soul mate. You two become one with all that there is. It's incredible. When I felt it, I knew I had to put it into a book to share the experience with my readers.

I would love to hear what you think. You can visit my Web site, www.loriwilde.com, or write to me at Lori Wilde, P.O. Box 31, Weatherford, TX 76086.

Lori Wilde

Books by Lori Wilde

HARLEQUIN BLAZE

Don't miss any of our special offers. Write to us at the following address for information on our newest releases.

Harlequin Reader Service
U.S.: 3010 Walden Ave., P.O. Box 1325, Buffalo, NY 14269
Canadian: P.O. Box 609, Fort Erie, Ont. L2A 5X3

GOTTA HAVE IT

Lori Wilde

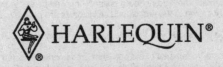

HARLEQUIN®

TORONTO • NEW YORK • LONDON
AMSTERDAM • PARIS • SYDNEY • HAMBURG
STOCKHOLM • ATHENS • TOKYO • MILAN • MADRID
PRAGUE • WARSAW • BUDAPEST • AUCKLAND

To Heather Rae
A very special person who'll one day soon
see her own book in print.
You've come a long way, baby.

ISBN 0-373-79156-9

GOTTA HAVE IT

Copyright © 2004 by Laurie Vanzura.

www.eHarlequin.com

Printed in U.S.A.

1

"YOU KNOW WHAT you need?"

"What?"

"To get plastered and pick up the first sexy stud who crosses your path. It's the best cure for those pesky just-got-stood-up-at-the-altar blues."

Abby Archer arrowed a glance at her best friend, Tess Baxter. They were seated side by side on wooden playground swings behind the church rectory. Abby was still wearing her eight-thousand-dollar ecru Vera Wang wedding gown and matching ballet style slippers, while Tess was dressed in a peach-colored spaghetti strap maid-of-honor dress and opened-toed sandals.

It was only then that Abby realized Tess's toenails were painted electric-neon-green. She couldn't help smiling at her quirky gal pal's choice of polish.

Tess wagged a bottle of Jose Cuervo Gold in one hand, a baggie of sliced limes in the other. "I've got the hooch, now let's go find us some stallions."

"Thanks for trying to cheer me up, but honestly I don't need to get drunk or have a one-night stand in order to salve my ego. Jilting me is the best thing Ken could have done for either one of us.''

''Will you just stop it?'' Tess twisted the top off the tequila and tossed it over her shoulder. The lid landed with a quiet plop onto ground still soft with the rare treat of an early-morning May rain in Phoenix.

''Stop what?''

''Making lemonade from lemons. You got ditched on your wedding day. You're entitled to be p.o'd.''

''Seriously, I'm cool with it. In fact…''

''In fact what?''

Abby lowered her voice, fidgeted with the powder-blue chantilly lace on the hanky she was supposed to have tucked into her pocket for something blue and admitted, ''I feel relieved.''

Tess made a derisive noise. ''Be that as it may, Ken humiliated you. If I'd gotten stood up, I'd hunt the guy down with a pickax and dispatch his manly parts. Chop, chop.''

''My best friend the drama queen,'' Abby said affectionately.

''Hey,'' Tess snapped her fingers. ''Do you want me to emasculate him for you? I volunteer to be your personal hit woman.''

''I appreciate the loyalty, but I think I'll let Ken keep his manly parts. He might need them for his future with Racy Racine.''

''I still can't believe he ran off with an exotic

dancer." Tess took a swig of the tequila, grimaced and bit down on a lime wedge. She extended the bottle to Abby and arched an eyebrow invitingly.

Abby shook her head and waved away the tequila. The swing's rusted metal chains creaked. "I just never expected Ken to do something so out of character. I mean the reason I was marrying him was because he was stable and predictable and reliable."

"And because your dad approved of him."

"That too."

"You know what? I think we oughta cash in your honeymoon tickets and go on a trip. You already have two weeks off and I'm in between jobs. Let's do something completely wild and crazy. Like drive to New Orleans and get our tongues pierced."

"Ouch! No!"

"Come on, I heard it enhances the sexual response," Tess cajoled.

Abby rolled her eyes. "You think everything enhances the sexual response."

"Well, if it doesn't it should."

"Sex is overrated."

Tess grinned impishly. "You're just saying that because you've never had great sex."

"I don't see what the big deal is."

Tess sighed and ran a hand through her short, spiky red hair. "Jeez Abby, don't you *ever* just allow yourself to get carried away by the moment?"

"You know how I feel about letting my emotions spill out of control. It's undignified and destructive."

"Come on, tell the truth. Somewhere deep down inside, when you were sleeping with Mr. Boring Buttoned-Down, didn't you fantasize about an explosive, passionate man who would sweep you off your feet, spirit you away to some mountain top and savagely ravage you?"

"Tess!"

"Just answer the question."

"Sometimes," Abby mumbled.

All the time, she thought to herself, and that was why she fought so hard to keep her sexual desires under wraps. She knew from experience the havoc unbridled passion wrought. Dark obsession scared the pants off her.

Tess's eyes lit up. "Do tell! Is he somebody famous? Or is your dream lover someone you know?"

"I don't really want to discuss this," Abby said, but a mental picture of Durango Creed immediately jumped into her head.

In her mind's eye he looked exactly as he had at eighteen when he had ridden out of her life forever. Black jeans, black leather jacket, black White Snake T-shirt, straddling his Ducati and begging her to run away with him. His ruggedly handsome face had glistened in the moonlight. His shoulder-length ebony hair was windblown, his black eyes deep and penetrating.

And his wicked, wicked smile had promised nothing but trouble.

He'd been the dead opposite of a knight in shining armor on a white charger.

In her daydreams, she longed for him to fulfill the promise inherent in his smile, but in reality, she'd sent him away without crossing that dangerous line. She had not acted on her impulses.

Thank God.

It was the smartest thing she'd ever done.

Or at least that was what she kept telling herself.

"This is the first time you've even hinted that you have secret sex dreams," Tess said. "You've been holding out. Fill me in, woman."

"It's silly. Illogical. And I should know better." Abby toed the dirt, staining her pristine white slipper with rich red Arizona soil. She knew she was ruining the shoes, but at this point, who cared?

"Abby, everyone has sex fantasies. It's normal. Honestly, I was beginning to think you were some kind of freak. It heartens me to hear you have a dream lover."

"Normal? For ten years? Even when you have a fiancé? It doesn't seem normal to me. I shouldn't have been fantasizing about anyone but Ken."

"If you had been fantasizing about Ken, you would be sitting here bawling your eyes out, brokenhearted over getting dumped."

"Maybe if I had been fantasizing about my nice

safe Ken, instead of some dangerous, long-ago hell-raiser, I wouldn't have gotten dumped.''

"Omigod.'' Tess clapped her hands with sudden glee. "Your midnight man is Durango Creed!''

"No, he's not,'' Abby lied quickly, and immediately had to raise her hanky to her nose to stay a sneeze.

"If your fantasy lover isn't Durango, then how come you're sneezing?''

"Because I have allergies.''

"That's bullshit and you know it. Whenever you deny your passion, you start sneezing.''

"No, I do not,'' Abby refuted her claim and promptly sneezed again.

"See what I mean? If you don't stop lying about your desires, you're gonna go into anaphylactic shock. Besides, it's nothing to be ashamed of, half the women in Phoenix had a jones for Durango.''

"Precisely why I didn't...I don't have a thing for him.'' Abby sneezed a third time.

"Me thinks thou doth sneeze too much.''

"Okay, all right. I did have a crush on him,'' Abby grumbled.

"Now was that so hard to confess?''

Yes. But at least she didn't sneeze again.

"Well, it really doesn't matter. I'm sure Durango Creed hates my guts. I was *such* a bitch to him.''

"Oh please, you've never been a bitch to anyone.''

"I refused to trust in him. I told him I couldn't

have a future with a common criminal." Even now the memory of the harsh words she'd been forced to say made her cringe with regret.

"You did it to protect yourself. What else could you do? And I'm sure he's gotten over you rejecting him by now. What was he thinking anyway? Giving you an ultimatum, expecting you to choose between him and your life in Silverton Heights?"

"He was hurt and confused. It was a real blow when his father remarried a woman half his age only four months after Durango's mother died. And then for his dad to take his new wife's side against his own son..." Abby let her sentence trail off.

"And it probably didn't help matters any when your dad had Durango thrown in the slammer for a week for vandalizing his stepmother's warehouse."

Abby shook her head. It had been a rough time in her life.

Yeah, and it was even rougher for Durango.

"Can we just drop this conversation, please?" she asked.

"Aw, just when I finally got your number? No wonder you're glad Ken ran off with Racy Racine. You're still in love with Durango."

"I was never in love with him," Abby denied, but her heart skipped a beat at her denunciation. "It was all teenage angst and hormones."

"Okay, then you're hot for him because he's the one you let get away."

"I'm not hot for him, dammit. It's just a stupid fantasy."

"Ooh, watch out," Tess teased. "Or you'll start sneezing again. Sure you don't want a shot of tequila?"

"Liquor is not the answer."

"Then what is?"

Abby doubled her arms across her chest. "I don't know."

"I do."

She shot Tess a sideways glance. "Well?"

"You gotta get it out of your system."

"Get what out of my system?"

"Durango."

Abby snorted. "Please."

"I'm serious. When he left town, you were left wondering what it would have been like if you two had hooked up. And you're probably still feeling guilty for hurting him the way you did, even though we both know you had no real choice."

"I couldn't have gone with him, Tess. I was only seventeen and my father was livid."

"I agree completely, but you've apparently spent the last ten years spinning this mental fantasy about him that no guy would be able to live up to, especially someone as dull as Ken. Ideally, the best way to exorcise the Durango demon would be to find the delectable Mr. Creed and screw his brains out."

"He's probably happily married with a backyard

full of cute kids who possess those same mesmerizing dark eyes.''

''No he's not.''

Abby frowned and her pulse quickened. ''How do you know that?''

''I saw an article on him in *Arizona* magazine a couple of months back. He's doing some kind of Outward Bound charity work for disaffected youths, and the reporter made a point of saying he was a very eligible bachelor.''

Abby covered her ears with her hands. She didn't want to hear any more. ''Let's not talk about him.''

''Okay, forget Durango. Then go find a surrogate and screw his brains out instead. Any wild, black-sheep bad boy should do the trick.''

Abby's heart hitched.

Tess's wacky solution actually made some sense. She *was* concerned about these incessant midnight fantasies she couldn't seem to shake. Obsessive fantasies that bothered her far more than she cared to admit.

She didn't want to feel this way. She wanted to free her mind of Durango so that the next time she found a stable, calm, sensible man she could give herself to him heart, mind and soul, the way she hadn't been able to give herself to Ken.

''I'm just not gutsy enough for a rowdy fling. You know me, Tess. I have to do a thorough consumer investigation before I change toothpastes. Can you actually see me hopping into bed with the first good-looking guy who nods my way?''

"Uh-oh," Tess warned. "Speaking of bed hopping, here comes Cassandra."

Abby sighed and watched her mother, who was wearing a skintight miniskirt and three-inch heels, take mincing steps across the playground toward them, a glass of champagne clutched in one hand, a skinny dark brown clove cigarette in the other.

"Well, at least she's minus the boy toy," Tess observed.

"Thank God for small favors."

"You know what?" Tess said, springing up off the swing as Abby's mother drew closer. "I think I'm going to call your travel agent about cashing in your honeymoon tickets to Aruba. We could take off tonight on an exciting adventure. Vegas, New Orleans, Miami. Let's cut loose. Whaddaya say?"

"I'd say you're just running off so you won't have to talk to Cassandra," Abby accused.

"Well, there is that." Tess grinned. "Want me to leave the tequila? You might need it."

"She'd probably just drink the entire thing."

"Good point." Tess tucked the bottle under her arm. "The tequila stays with me."

Tess and Cassandra gave each other fake smiles as they passed. For some reason her best friend and her mother rubbed each other the wrong way. Abby had never said anything to either one of them, but she'd always figured their animosity toward each other stemmed from the fact that they were two peas in a pod, both of them flamboyant, impulsive and audacious.

"Hi, sweetie." Her mother, smelling of her signature honeysuckle cologne and the clove cigarette, plunked down on the swing Tess had just vacated.

"Hello, Cassandra."

She reached over and gently touched Abby's shoulder. "You can call me Mom today, if you want."

Abby shook her head. After her mother had left her father, she'd insisted Abby call her Cassandra so the guys she dated wouldn't know she was old enough to have an eight-year-old daughter. As Abby grew older, Cassandra raided her closet for hip clothes and flirted with Abby's boyfriends.

All except for Durango. Abby had never introduced him to her mother.

"How you holdin' up?" Cassandra polished off her champagne and then set the flute on top of the adjoining slide.

"I'm doing okay."

"Your father seems to be having a rough time of it. He's apologizing to the guests like he's the one who did something wrong."

"Ken was his campaign manager and now he's going to have to fire him. That's causing him grief. Plus, Daddy feels responsible because he was the one who got us together and he really likes Ken."

"Yeah well, birds of a feather," her mother muttered.

"Please, don't even go there."

"You're right. No need to get petty, but I'm betting your father lost the sticker price of a showroom BMW on this failed shindig. And I'm going to give him the benefit of the doubt and pretend he's more worried about you than how this is going to reflect on him with the voting public."

Abby poked her tongue against the inside of her cheek. She'd had years of practice mediating truces and cease-fires between her parents. That skill had actually been excellent training for her job as a public relations specialist for a large nonprofit organization and she'd learned her lessons well. She refused to rise to Cassandra's dangling bait.

"Nobody cares that I got stood up. Daddy's running for governor, not me. And you needn't worry about the cost of the wedding." *As if her mother would.* "Daddy took out wedding insurance."

"But of course he did." Her mother gave a dry laugh and took a drag of her cigarette. "Wayne is nothing if not sensible."

She said "sensible" as if it was a dirty word.

They sat in silence. Her mother smoking, Abby kicking more dirt onto her slippers.

"You wanna go shoe shopping or something?" Cassandra asked. Bonding over a sale on Manolo Blahniks was her mother's answer to everything.

"I'm doing okay." Abby forced a smile. "Honest. You can go back to Tahoe with Tad, guilt free."

"It's Tab, darling."

"Whatever."

Her mother reached over and brushed a lock of hair away from Abby's forehead. "Ken wasn't right for you. You do know that."

"I think I sort of got the clue when he didn't show up at the altar."

"You are much too passionate for a dullard like him, my dear."

"Apparently Ken isn't all that dull. He caught Racy Racine's attention."

Cassandra waved a hand. "That won't last. The stripper is just out for his money. Soon as she discovers he's as exciting as watching paint dry she'll abscond with his wallet and he'll come crawling back to you. But don't you dare take him back. Like I said, you're much too lusty for the likes of him."

Abby laughed humorlessly. "Yeah, right. I'm so lusty even dull Ken deserted me."

"You just hide your passion because you're scared that if you let yourself go you'll turn out like me."

"I'm not like you. Not in the least," Abby protested, and then she sneezed.

"Deny it all you want, sugar babe. That sneeze says it all."

"I have allergies!"

"Then how come you only sneeze when the topic of conversation turns to passionate feelings?"

"I sneeze at other times."

"Do you really?"

"Yes." No.

Cassandra just smiled knowingly. "Like it or not, my hot Gypsy blood courses through your veins and those sneeze attacks are nature's way of trying to get you to realize it."

Abby thought of Durango and a flame of fear leaped into her heart. Could it be true? Was she sitting on a volcano of passion that was just waiting to erupt and spew disaster on everyone in her path?

She swallowed. "It's nothing a good antihistamine won't cure."

"You wish. Truth is, you're just aching to express your secret inner desires. Deep down inside, you know that's the case."

"You're wrong. I have no secret inner desires," Abby fibbed, and crinkled her nose to keep from sneezing.

"Then why do you have Tess for a friend."

"Because I like her."

"And why do you like her?"

"Because she's fun."

"Exactly. You made her your best friend so you can live through her vicariously. She does all the things you're afraid to do and you tag along. But sooner or later, no matter how hard you try to sublimate it, that passion of yours is going to come bursting out. Just like it did with me.''

"Not if I refuse to give in to it.''

"It's bigger than your will, darling. God knows I tried to be a good wife to Wayne and a good mother to you. I tried to live the suburban lifestyle, but it just wasn't possible. I felt suffocated, smothered, invisible. I had to be me and I won't apologize for that.''

"You don't have to justify yourself.''

"I'm not justifying myself. Don't you get it? I'm trying to warn you.''

"Warn me?''

"Once you open that Pandora's box, Abby, once your true passion is released, watch out. There's no going back.''

"So what you're saying is that I'm correct in suppressing my impulsive, irrational desires in favor of calm, cool, calculated objectivity.''

"No, what I'm saying is that sooner or later you're going to have to face up to who you really are. And when you do, you'll stop having 'allergies.' Sooner or later something has to give. You can't keep trying to be this perfect person just to please your father.''

"You're so off base it's laughable.''

"Am I?''

"Yes.''

"Then prove it,'' her mother challenged.

"Prove it?'' Abby blinked. What was Cassandra talking about?

"Let yourself go. Do something wild and crazy and uninhibited."

"Wild and crazy and uninhibited," Abby echoed.

"Yes. Clear it up in your mind. Establish once and for all that you're not like me," Cassandra continued. "Go on a trip where you don't know anyone and make a complete fool of yourself. Pick up a stranger. Have great sex. Emulate Tess."

"There's no need for that."

"Really? Are you trying to tell me you're not plagued by secret fantasies of breaking loose, breaking out, breaking away?"

Abby swallowed but did not answer.

"Give it a shot. If I'm wrong and you're not this passionate naughty girl trapped in a good girl's body, then nothing bad will happen. You'll come home with some nice memories, you'll resume your safe, stable life and you can rest peaceful in the knowledge that passion will never induce you to run out on your husband and kid."

"I'll keep that in mind. Thanks for your input." She sat on her hands because she didn't want Cassandra to see they were trembling. "Your motherly advice is incredibly valuable at this stage of my life."

"Why, Abby, are you being sarcastic?" Her mother looked amused.

"Sorry, I've had a bad day."

"Don't back off now. Stand up for yourself. Let me have it. Show some passion."

But Abby wasn't about to give her mother the satisfaction of losing her composure. "Have a safe trip home."

"I'm being dismissed?" Her mother's grin widened, and she got to her feet and retrieved her empty champagne glass.

"I love you, Mom," Abby said. "But we'll never see eye to eye on this issue."

"Oh you dear, sweet, innocent girl." Cassandra dropped a dry kiss on her cheek, then turned and sashayed away, leaving the scent of honeysuckle and cloves lingering on Abby's skin.

Two minutes after her mother had returned to the rectory, Tess came bouncing back outside, beaming like a flood lamp and waving a piece of paper in her hand. "I found us the perfect getaway spot."

With a sinking sensation, Abby wondered if they would be shooting craps in Vegas or getting smashed on hurricanes in the French Quarter or mamboing with Latin lovers in Miami.

Could she do this? Should she do this? Would she do this?

Abby sneezed delicately into her lace hanky, and the parting words that Ken had spoken when he'd called to tell her he wasn't showing up for the wedding echoed in her ears.

"You're just not fiery enough, Abby. Look at you. If you were emotionally committed to me, you'd be jealous of Racine and scratching my eyes out for

*treating you this way. Instead you're telling me it's
okay. That's what's wrong with us. Why I can't marry
you. No fire.''*

And then she heard Tess say, *''The best way to
exorcise the Durango demon would be to find the delectable Mr. Creed and screw his brains out.''*

And lastly came her mother's dangerous challenge.
*''Let yourself go. Do something wild and crazy. Prove
once and for all you're not like me.''*

Part of her wanted to accept the dare. Take a risk.
Vanquish her fantasies.

But part of her was terrified. What if her mother
was right? What if they *were* alike?

''Earth to Abby.'' Tess snapped her fingers in front
of Abby's face.

''Huh?''

''Don't you want to know where we're going?''

Abby closed her eyes and braced herself for the
worst. ''Lay it on me.''

''A week of total pampering at the Tranquility Spa
in Sedona.''

Abby opened one eye and peeked at her friend.
''Sedona? Really?''

''Uh-huh.''

''You're not kidding me? Serene, slow-paced Sedona? With the soothing red rock mesas and inspi-
rational vortices?''

''I figured peace and quiet was really what you
were looking for.''

Love for her friend overwhelmed her. This was exactly the kind of regenerative trip she needed. She didn't require endless thrills or excitement. She didn't have to act wild and reckless in order to prove herself. All she needed was a calm place where she could relax and get some perspective on her life.

She jumped off the swing and enveloped Tess in a big hug. "Thank you. Thank you so much."

"Hey," Tess said, "what are friends for?"

"But what about you? You wanted fun and excitement and to get laid."

"Well." Tess grinned. "*My* fantasy lover, Colin Cruz, happens to be making a movie in Sedona. I was hoping we could watch them film. Plus, you know what I heard?" She lowered her voice.

"What?"

"The electromagnetic energy in Sedona intensifies orgasmic pleasure."

"You're kidding."

"Apparently, there's no sex like vortex sex."

2

"GOOD MORNING, HANDSOME," the low, husky voice of Sunrise Jeep Tours dispatcher Connie Vargas oozed from the two-way radio on the dashboard.

"Morning, Connie." Durango Creed grinned. Connie was sixty-five if she was a day, but she flirted like she was sixteen. He admired the woman's spirit. She didn't let her age slow her down. "Did you sleep well?"

"Not too well, cowboy." Mischief sparkled in her tone. "You weren't in my bed."

"Connie, believe me, I wouldn't be able to keep up with you."

She chuckled. "Yeah, right. I've heard the rumors about you."

"Lies, all lies."

Connie snorted indelicately. "What about the flock of city girls who come here and personally request you as their guide? You tryin' to tell me you don't offer any additional services that aren't part of our regular tour package?"

Durango pretended to be offended. "Are you impugning my virtue?"

"No, but I think your next customers might give your virtue a run for its money."

"Oh?"

"You've got a pickup at Tranquility Spa. Name's Baxter, party of two for the private Vortex Tour and the lady specifically asked for Durango Creed. She sounded very sexy too."

"I'm on it."

"I'm sure you are, cowboy. Over and out."

With a shake of his head, Durango grinned and wheeled his bright orange Jeep up the narrow L'Auberge Lane and then headed west toward the secluded, chichi health spa. He blew past the Black Cow Café, the warm desert wind stirring both his hair and his blood, and hung a right at the split.

From his peripheral vision, he caught a glimpse of Cathedral Rock jutting proud and majestic in the distance. The sun, filtering in and out through the shifting clouds. made it appear as if the formation was in motion, a subtle, graceful dance of light and shadows. The sight of those mesas never failed to rouse something primal inside Durango.

A motorcycle came up on his left. He turned his head. The sound of the bike's engine captured his attention. When he saw it was a Ducati he found himself thinking about Abby Archer, and a double twist of wistful longing and downright horniness knotted his gut like a pretzel.

Without any difficulty at all, he could still picture

how she looked the last time he had seen her. Standing on the balcony of her father's palatial house, wearing a thin white sheath that in the moonlight showed off every inch of her nubile seventeen-year-old body. Her dark hair, which was usually pulled back in a sleek ponytail, was hanging loose about her shoulders, her breasts rising high and firm, her creamy skin gleaming seductively.

God, she'd been something special. Just like Sedona herself. Beautiful, calm, tranquil on the surface but underneath ran all that raw passionate energy. Maybe that's why he had ended up in Sedona. He'd always been a sucker for the fire-and-ice paradox.

And if he and Abby had ever fully explored the chemistry surging between them, they probably would have spontaneously combusted.

But she'd told him she didn't trust him. That he was too wild, too untamed, too reckless for her. The tears shining in her eyes had belied her words, but he'd had no choice other than to leave her behind.

Durango exhaled. It was just as well nothing had happened between them. Even though they came from the same privileged world, she fit in and he never did. As evidenced by the very different paths they'd elected to walk. Abby had stayed with the tried and true and he had chosen the road less traveled.

It's just that every once in a while, he couldn't help wondering what if?

He turned down the secluded driveway to the spa

and slowed long enough to flash his pass when he reached the security gate. The guard waved him inside and he motored around to the front entrance.

Two women stood under the awning. One was a skinny redhead dressed in funky, punky threads and high-heeled sandals that were totally inappropriate for hiking the mesa trails.

Mentally he rolled his eyes. *Tourists.*

The other woman was a breathtaking brunette who wore a pair of classy tailored white shorts, a red V-necked tee that enhanced her gorgeous breasts and a sensible pair of walking shoes that, in spite of their ordinary construction made her legs look extraordinary. Pricey designer sunglasses covered her eyes and a large straw hat held back her hair and shaded her face from the sun.

His mouth watered.

Strangely enough, the brunette looked a lot like Abby. She had the same full lips, same proud tilt of the head and the same dimpled chin. Maybe that's why he was instantly attracted.

Something in his chest tugged.

Trick of the light and his imagination. He'd been thinking about Abby and now he was seeing her. He killed the engine and climbed from the Jeep to find out if they were Baxter, party of two.

He approached the redhead. "Hello, I'm with Sunrise Tours, did you ladies arrange for a—"

He broke off when the brunette inhaled sharply

with a soft, well-bred sound. Quickly she reached up and snatched off her sunglasses.

His heart hammered and his palms went slick with sweat as he peered into those familiar hazel eyes.

It *is* Abby, he thought, at the same moment she whispered, "Durango Creed."

FROM THE MOMENT she spied Durango's long, lean muscular body swinging out of the Jeep, Abby knew she'd been set up.

"Tess Baxter, what have you done?" she hissed through clenched teeth.

"Consider this my thank-God-the-wedding-didn't-go-off present to you." Tess laughed.

Before Abby had time to tell her that she was *sooo* dead for pulling this stunt, Durango was filling her direct field of vision with his breathtaking presence. The man was more impressive than the incredible red rock formations surrounding them.

All Abby had wanted was to come to Sedona, get a massage, maybe take a mud bath or two and have an expert facial. Her goal was to relax and regroup after getting ditched at the altar by her fiancé. But one look in those unforgettable eyes and everything changed.

She felt something shake loose in her chest, like a tearing away sensation.

Omigod, here he is, here he is in the flesh.

She curled her fingers into her fists at her sides and forced herself to breathe normally.

The years had been far more than kind. In fact, time had been embarrassingly generous. He had fully matured, his teenaged shoulders and thighs broadening into manhood. Yet he still wore that cocky, defensive bad-boy stance like a mantle of pride. His face was fuller, less rangy than it had been, but his waist was just as narrow. His hair, long and bound back in a short ponytail, was just as dark and thick. His eyes just as impossibly black.

And wicked.

He was even more gorgeous than before.

Her pulse took off, galloping like a high-spirited Thoroughbred on the last furlough of the Kentucky Derby. She stifled the urge to flee from the intensity of those eyes, which seemed to possess a secret, sinister wisdom all their own.

Then an equally compelling craving had her longing to fling herself into his arms with an ease born of intimate knowledge.

But she did neither.

Five years in the public relations business and twenty-seven years as the daughter of an influential judge had taught her how to sweep her true feelings aside in favor of the politically correct response. Abby thrust out her hand, pasted an artificial smile on her face and repeated his name.

"Well, well, well," he said, ignoring her outstretched palm and sinking his hands onto his low-slung hips. "If it isn't Angel Archer."

Angel.

The sound of his old nickname for her stirred Abby inexplicably. She'd forgotten he used to call her that because she was such a Goody Two-shoes.

She stood there with her hand thrust out, feeling like a fool and not knowing how to gracefully retract it. She had the oddest sensation that if she just stretched her hand out far enough she could caress that night ten years ago, touch the girl she had once been and pull her back from making the terrible mistake of sending him away.

Fanciful, decried the critic in her head. *You can't recapture the past.*

Grab him, whispered her long-buried desire. *Make a new future.*

And there lay the crux of her predicament. Safety on one side, passion on the other and Abby trapped firmly in the middle, immobilized.

Durango sized her up with one long, lingering glance that made her feel completely naked. She didn't like feeling vulnerable. She didn't like feeling out of control. And he made her feel both of these things.

Her nose itched.

Thank heavens, she'd taken an antihistamine on the drive up, even if it did make her mouth all cottony. It was better than sneezing her head off.

"After all these years, you still remember me," he said.

"Of course she remembers you," Tess babbled. "She still has sex dreams about you and—"

Abby trod on Tess's instep. *Shh.*

"Ow!" Tess glared and hopped around on one foot, grossly exaggerating the slight injury.

Abby sent her a look that said, *serves you right for interfering in my love life.*

Durango's grin widened. "And you were going to be satisfied with just shaking my hand? You haven't changed a bit, Angel. Still holding back. Still keeping your emotions under wraps."

"I don't think that's…" Abby began, but got no further.

"Come 'ere." He strode forward, encircled her in a bear hug and lifted her off her feet.

Oh, my.

Contact with his hard, masculine body threw her into a tailspin. Her breasts were smashed flat against his broad, honed chest. He smelled delightfully of wind and sun and leather.

His muscles rippled as he squeezed her tight. His hair tickled her ear. His chin made contact with her cheek and the slight scrape of beard stubble shoved her long-dormant libido into overdrive.

She wanted him.

Badly.

Abby froze. She remembered now, with distinct

clarity, why she hadn't taken his side all those years ago when everyone in Silverton Heights had turned against him.

She'd been too afraid.

The strength of his life force was just too overwhelming, his passion too raw, his intensity too intimidating for her to handle. She had been the good girl with the stark dread of ending up bad, just like her incorrigible mother.

Durango kept holding her. His big laugh rumbled intoxicatingly in her ears, his ebony eyes sparkling with devilment, his exhilarating scent blinding her to any other smell.

No.

She would not allow herself to get swept away by the force of his energy. She would just wait him out. Eventually he would have to put her feet back on the ground.

It was like waiting out a hurricane.

He just kept standing there. Holding her.

Abby didn't move. She most certainly did not hug him in return, but his embrace transported her back in time.

In her mind's eye, she saw the sexually repressed young girl she had once been longing to explore the red-hot passion surging through her veins but was too scared to act. That's why she'd kept fantasizing about Durango all these years. Because he was the flame she hadn't been brave enough to extinguish.

At last, Durango set her down and stepped away to eye her once more.

"You look amazing," he said huskily.

She dropped her gaze. *So do you,* she yearned to say but prudently murmured, "Thank you."

"You still living in Phoenix?" His face was lively with interest, his body language compelling.

"Uh-huh."

"She's still living in her father's house." Tess rolled her eyes. "Of course, she was getting married, but that deal sort of fell through. The groom ditched her for a stripper on their wedding day. Thank heavens. Ken was all wrong for her."

"Ken Rockford?" Durango cleared his throat.

At the private high school in Silverton Heights that they'd all three attended, Durango and Ken had been archenemies, with Ken the class president and football quarterback to Durango's rebel without a cause, smoking in the boys' room.

Abby nodded but didn't look at him. Gee thanks, Tess, for making things so much more awkward.

Durango snorted but said nothing. An uncomfortable silence fell.

"I'm Tess, by the way." Tess stepped forward to shake his hand. "Remember me? I was away at boarding school when you and Abby were dating, but we met at your father's annual Christmas party that year."

"Didn't you used to be a blonde?" he asked.

"Yep, and a brunette before that and once I did the tricolor blond-brunette-red-hair thing. So I guess you could say I was a calico." She shrugged. "I'm not like Abby who's had the same tame hairstyle all her life. I get bored easily."

Durango laughed. "I like you, Tess."

"I like you too, Durango."

Dammit, was Tess flirting with him? And criticizing her hairdo to boot? Abby experienced a flick of jealousy so hot and quick it startled her.

"Are we going to do this vortex thing or not?" she snapped, irritated with herself because she sounded jealous.

"Sure, sure." Durango nodded. "Who's calling shotgun?"

"Abby is!" Tess said.

"Or we could both just sit in the back."

"No, no, you two need to catch up on old times," Tess announced, and shoved Abby toward the passenger side of the Jeep.

"No, really, there's no need. I'm happy with the back," Abby argued.

But Durango was getting behind the wheel and Tess was sprawled out across the back seat.

Move over, Abby mouthed silently.

Tess shook her head.

Abby waggled her finger at her. *I'm going to get even with you for this.*

Saucily, Tess stuck out her tongue.

Durango started the engine, leaving Abby no choice except to climb into the passenger seat beside him.

She stopped short when she spied a credo medallion dangling from the rearview mirror. The silver lettering against the red background caught the sun and glinted enticingly.

Freefall, it read.

Freefall. Didn't that just about sum up Durango? And her fantasies concerning him.

Her dreams always involved an element of danger and risk. In her reveries, he was usually a virile pirate or a black-hearted bandit or a lawless mercenary.

She remembered his hot kisses, how they'd both frightened and thrilled her. She recalled the way his fevered hand had felt sliding up underneath her shirt, expertly unhooking her bra. She recollected how he'd shocked her young sensibilities by pressing the length of his male hardness against her yearning thigh. She could not forget the way her heart had pounded and how much it had scared her. This desperate wanting.

And it appeared nothing had changed!

I am not giving in to desire. I'm not like my mother. I'm a controlled person. I am. I am. I am. This had been her solemn mantra in high school and it was still her mantra now.

So why did she suddenly feel like she was in an irrevocable tailspin?

Abby sneezed into a tissue and then fastened her

seat belt. She dropped her hands into her lap and struggled to get her heart rate under control. She had had no concept that seeing Durango again would affect her so profoundly.

Of course if she hadn't been ambushed by Tess's subterfuge, she would have been more prepared for their meeting, more in control of her emotions, more patient with her distressing reaction. She shot a glance back at her wily friend, who had her face tilted up to the morning sun and was grinning one of those sneaky Cheshire-cat grins of hers.

And damn if she wasn't softly humming, Sheryl Crow's "All I Wanna Do."

Abby knew the message Tess was sending. Just relax and have some fun. But how could she relax when her entire world had just tilted off its axis?

Durango put the Jeep in gear, shot around the paved circular driveway and out of the gate. Abby clutched at her hat to keep it from flying off. She could literally feel his sexual energy.

The man was potent. She had to give him that. Testosterone shimmered off him in waves.

But did she really want to explore his…um… potency?

The chemistry was still there. No denying. Bubbling, sizzling, churning. Scarier than ever.

You know that's why you want him. Because he's not safe. Because he is taboo.

Good grief. Why was Cassandra's voice tap-dancing around in her head?

She could feel the current of sexuality swirling around them, a compelling nexus of desire. But was a wild fling really the answer to ending the sexual fantasies she could not shake? Or would seducing this man open up a whole new can of hurt?

She slipped her sunglasses back on and coolly said, "So what exactly is a vortex?"

He turned his head to smile at her, and her heart, which had just begun to settle down, kicked back into high gear. If the man could bottle that grin the world's fuel problems would be solved.

"Essentially it's the energy of the earth."

"Ooookay."

"The energy can be magnetic, electric or electro-magnetic. The magnetic vortices are considered masculine, the feminine are electric and the electromagnetic are neutral."

"Which one of those are we going to?" Abby asked, and caught herself studying his large, masculine hands as he clutched the steering wheel.

He had such nice, long, broad fingers. She recollected how those same fingers had once tickled the underside of her throat while his hot, wet tongue had eagerly explored her ear.

Magnetic, indeed.

"We're going to Cathedral Rock first. It's a feminine vortex."

"What's supposed to happen there?"

"Maybe nothing." Durango shrugged. "It all depends on what you're looking for. Some people come to Sedona for spiritual growth. Others arrive searching for health and emotional well-being. Still others find themselves at a crossroad in their lives and they're seeking guidance. Sedona is a good place to turn inward and find out what you really want."

That's me. I'm at a crossroad.

And she had no idea what it was she really wanted out of life.

"What kind of guidance can these earth energies give you?" she asked, her curiosity piqued.

"If you let yourself feel the power, they can guide you anywhere you want to go."

"Sounds cryptic," Tess piped up.

"It's an individual experience. If you're attuned, the vortex can lead you to balance and harmony in your life. Or it can point the way to an important career change. It can help you in your relationships or it can set you on the path to heightened awareness."

"What about sex?" Tess asked.

"I'm for it," Durango said.

Tess giggled. "Me too. But what I've heard is that vortex energy can enhance your sex life."

Durango chuckled. His laugh was low and sensuous and snaked a fissure of that very heightened awareness right up Abby's spinal column. "If that's what you need. Sure, why not?"

"I'm betting the electromagnetic vortices are the sexiest, right?" Tess sat up and leaned over the front seat.

"I never really thought of it that way," Durango said. "But, yeah, I suppose those would be considered the sexiest vortices. Concurrent flow and all that."

"Do you really believe the vortices have such influential power?" Abby asked.

"Not at all," he said. "The power is within you. The vortex is just a channel, funneling energy into whatever you bring to it. Positive or negative. Light or dark. Passionate or dispassionate."

Abby swallowed. "All this sounds pretty out there. New Agey. Weird."

And not at all like the old Durango she used to know. That young rebel had been full of torment and anger. He was different now. More relaxed, more philosophical, more sure of his place in the world. Plus, he didn't seem to hold the slightest grudge against her for turning against him all those years ago. That was really nice. She approved of the changes in him.

Durango leaned over and placed the flat of his broad thumb in the center of her forehead. "Open your mind, Abby. The world is a much bigger place than your father's circle of influence."

She stared at him, her forehead tingling from his touch. "What's that supposed to mean?"

"You figure it out." Durango's enigmatic black eyes challenged her to go beyond the tried-and-true. He was so busy watching her that he missed his turn-off and had to corner quickly.

The tires squealed. Abby sucked in her breath and clutched the hand rest.

The credo medallion flew off the rearview mirror and dropped into her lap.

Freefall.

With shaky fingers, Abby slipped the medallion back over the mirror.

"Yee-ha!" Tess said from the back seat. "That was fun."

"Just checking to see if you were awake," Durango joked.

They turned down Back O' Beyond Road. It seemed an appropriate name encircled as they were by miles and miles of the majestic red rocks. Abby had to admit there was something incredibly special about those rock mesas. No matter what you were doing, you invariably felt your eyes drawn to them.

There were other Jeeps on the road. Other tours. They drove for a while longer and then Durango found a place to park.

"We walk from here," he said, strapping on his backpack.

The weather was temperate. A good fifteen degrees

cooler than in Phoenix. The sun was bright but not overpowering. The air was peaceful. Quiet.

Abby couldn't believe that she had lived out her entire life in Phoenix and had never once made the short two-hour trek to Sedona. She didn't have much time for vacations. She stayed too busy with her job and running her father's household and helping out with his political campaigns. And whenever she did take time off, she usually preferred cruising the Caribbean to checking out local hot spots.

Just think, all this time, Durango was only two hours away and you never knew.

Her heart lurched oddly. Why did that realization make her feel so sad?

The world is a much bigger place than your father's circle of influence. Durango's words echoed in her head.

He led the way up the trail. They'd only gone half a mile before Tess started bitching. "How come nobody told me there'd be so much walking."

"I did suggest you might not want to wear high-heeled sandals." Abby shook her head.

"But hiking shoes blow my sexy image." Tess pouted.

"It's not too much farther," Durango said.

"Why don't they build roads right up to the vortex?" Tess whined. "For us couch potatoes."

"That would kinda ruin the whole point of nature," Abby pointed out.

They passed a few other hikers on their trek up the rock. Tess finally ended up pulling off her shoes and padding after them barefoot. The sound of her feet slapping against the red sandstone echoed softly throughout the canyon.

When they came to a large flat rock in the middle of the path, Tess plunked herself down on it.

"You guys go ahead." She waved a hand. "I just wanna sit here and rest a minute."

"We'll wait with you," Abby said and perched beside her. The last thing she wanted to do was be alone with Durango.

"I really want to be by myself. To meditate."

Abby stared at her. "Since when do you meditate?"

"Since I found out Colin Cruz is deep into Eastern philosophy. Now, do you mind?" Tess made shooing motions at them. "Scram."

She knew what her friend was up to and, while Tess thought she had her best interest at heart, Abby wasn't the least bit grateful.

"Abby?" Durango raised a questioning eyebrow and cocked his head in the direction of the summit. "How 'bout we give Tess some space."

Okay, fine. Blowing out her breath, Abby slid off the rock and reluctantly followed Durango up the trail. So much for the quiet, tranquil buttes of Sedona.

"You and Tess are total opposites," Durango said

to Abby when they were out of earshot. "How have you stayed friends for so long?"

"Tess is something of a character," Abby conceded. "She's a lot of fun to be around."

"And you're the ground wire."

"I guess you could say that."

They reached the top and, just as they were going up, a camera-wielding, balding, paunchy, middle-aged man wearing Bermuda shorts, a Van Halen T-shirt and black sandals with plaid socks was coming down.

"I looked all over this damned rock and couldn't find hide nor hair of that stupid vortex," he was muttering under his breath.

"A vortex isn't something you see," Durango told him. "It's an energy field. You have to feel it."

The guy snorted, mumbled something about New Age fruitcakes and took off down the trail.

"Well, he was friendly," Abby said. "Not."

"People like him show up all the time. They're usually from a big city. Rushed, in a hurry, looking for a short cut to inner peace. They hear about the restorative power of the vortex and they think it's a ticket to instant enlightenment. But there's no such thing."

Abby cocked her head and studied him. He looked at peace and she was happy for him. "You seem to have come a long way in the enlightenment department."

"Hey, it was either get peaceful or drive myself nuts holding on to grudges."

"Did you have a grudge against me?" she dared to ask him.

"What do you think?"

"I'm thinking yes."

He nodded. "I was pretty hurt at the time. I thought we were working on something special, but it turned out I was wrong. Just goes to show you how foolish teenagers can be."

"Not totally foolish," she said huskily.

"No?"

"I thought we were working on something special, too."

He eyed her speculatively. "But when the going got tough and you got going…"

"What can I say?" She shrugged and tried not to let him see how much her lack of faith in him still bothered her. "I was a scared kid."

"You're not a kid anymore."

"No."

"But you're still scared." There was that grin of his again, more wicked than ever.

The sun beat down. The air was alive with electricity. Abby felt something then. She didn't know if it was the famous vortex energy or if it was energy of a much more tangible kind, but her skin prickled and her nerve endings tingled.

Durango's chest was rising and falling in a rapid rhythm that matched her own edgy breathing.

A tangle of complicated emotions skirled inside her, spiraling outward in an expanding circle, drawing her to him.

Their eyes met and the moment was straight out of some romantic movie. His gaze locked with hers and Abby couldn't catch her breath. Her chest literally hurt with the intensity of wanting him.

The vortex was sucking her in. Pulling her down into a place she wasn't so sure she wanted to go.

Run! Run! cried the cautious side she'd inherited from her father.

Stay, stay, inveigled her mother's Gypsy blood.

''Durango,'' she whispered.

''Angel.''

He reached for her.

She walked toward him.

He wet his lips.

She pursed hers.

He took off her hat.

She looked into his face.

Oh wow, oh boy, oh no.

And Abby just knew he would have kissed her if she hadn't picked that moment to start sneezing.

3

WHAT IN THE HADES *do you think you're pulling,
Creed?*

Oh, he knew what he was doing and it wasn't good.
In fact, he had very, very bad intentions.

When Durango had first realized that the sleek-
haired brunette on the steps of the Tranquility Spa
was none other than Abby Archer, the teenage crush
who had busted his heart by siding with their snobby,
high-society community against him, his first despi-
cable thought had been—*I've gotta get even.*

His second, more mature thought had been—*I've
gotta let it go.*

Ten years had passed. He rarely thought about her
anymore and he'd made a great life for himself here
in Sedona. And yet a touch of that young rebel re-
mained. A bit of his heart was still hardened against
her and the collective of Silverton Heights.

He wasn't proud of his feelings but neither could
he dismiss them. He felt what he felt. Good or bad.

Yet how could he blame her for what had happened? Abby had done what she had to do in order
to live with herself. She'd been a suppressed seven-

teen-year-old girl with a powerful father. She'd had little choice but to accept his edict. Rationally, Durango understood that.

But deep down inside he was still the vulnerable kid who didn't quite comprehend why he hadn't been enough for her.

Besides, his real beef had been with her old man.

And his own.

Durango grit his teeth at the memory. Although he had long since gotten over being disowned in favor of his father's calculating trophy wife, he still couldn't fathom why Phillip Creed had chosen to believe his stepmother Meredith's outrageous lie that Durango had attempted to force her to have sex with him, when it had been the other way around.

Meredith had come on to *him*.

Durango tried telling his father the accusation was a ruse on Meredith's part because he'd discovered she was hiding illicit business dealings at her company where his father had just bought part interest.

But his father had sunk even lower, allowing Meredith to intimidate him into involving his buddy, Judge Archer, in the private family matter. His father persuaded Abby's dad to jail him for a week, when in a desperate bid to be heard, Durango had lashed out and vandalized one of Meredith's warehouses.

The memory of those seven days behind bars would stay with him forever.

Let it go. Water under the bridge. He was happy now and that's all that mattered.

Then Durango's third and most compelling thought had been—*Damn, but Abby's hot. I've gotta find a way to get her into my bed.*

Now, standing here atop Cathedral Rock, gazing into her soulful hazel eyes and lusting after those full cherry-colored lips, he was thinking—*You still haven't found your passion, have you sweetheart?*

He could see she was lost and she didn't even know it. His heart literally ached and his weakness for her bothered the hell out of him.

Why did he still care?

Abby was the same person she'd been a decade ago. As evidenced by the fact she had almost married that candy-assed Ken Rockford. Still kowtowing to her father, still denying her fire, still hiding from her true self.

He'd seen the depth in her from the beginning, even though she'd never seen it in herself.

The first time he laid eyes on Abby, he'd been serving out detention in the library, when she'd ambled through the door wearing a matching sweater set and clutching her books to her chest. Every hair was in place, her skirt ironed, understated makeup, tasteful jewelry. She'd looked like some kind of throwback to the nineteen fifties.

Prim, proper, perfect. All except for those full, sensuous lips and the provocative way her hips rolled when she walked.

Those lips and that walk gave away the inner woman. On the surface she might be calm, controlled and composed but underneath, oh underneath, she was just waiting to spring free.

Fire and ice.

But nothing had changed for her. Abby's body was ripe with unexplored sexuality, begging for release. He could see it in the way she moistened her lips when he looked at her mouth. He could smell it in the estrogen rising up off her skin. He could hear it in her soft sneeze whenever he stared at her with open desire.

He longed to show her that a life without passion wasn't worth living. He yearned to teach her how to listen to her own desires and ignore the opinions of others. He hungered to ruffle her cool aplomb and show her exactly what she'd been missing.

"What are you seeking, Abby?" he asked, searching her face.

A part of him truly wanted to help her find herself, but another part of him couldn't keep from thinking how tasty it would be to pull her down on top of the red sandstone, whisk those fancy white shorts over her womanly hips and show her right then and there what she'd been missing.

His pulse thundered and his abdominal muscles tugged. What was the matter with him? If he'd wanted revenge, he should have taken it ten years ago. Too much time had passed to dredge up ancient history.

"Passion got you scared?" he asked.

"Excuse me?" She blinked.

"You sneezed."

"So what?"

"You used to start sneezing whenever things got too hot to handle."

"Why does everyone keep saying that to me?"

"Maybe because it's true."

"It's not true! I have allergies."

"Yeah, you're allergic to digging too deep and finding out what's really going on inside your heart."

She stared at him. He'd caught her off guard. Good. She needed to be unsettled more often. Just as he was unsettled.

"What are you searching for?" he repeated.

"Um…" She hesitated. "Who says I'm searching for anything?"

"Most people come to Sedona on a quest."

"I'm simply on vacation."

"Is that true? Or are you here to lick your wounds after getting dumped at the altar by Ken Rockford?" He really hadn't meant to get that dig in, it had just slipped out.

Okay, I'm jealous. So sue me.

"I'm not heartbroken over losing Ken, if that's

what you're asking. In fact, that's the problem. I can't seem to feel anything monumental.''

He wanted to ask if Ken had ever made her sneeze. Instead, he said, ''I know how to cure your problem.''

''Oh, you do?'' She raised one of her cool, perfectly arched eyebrows. How well he remembered that haughty high-society-princess look. It goaded him to take action. ''And how is that?''

He meant to tell her she needed to let go and do something reckless for once in her life, but the way she held herself aloof and regal made him itch to bring her down a peg or two.

''Like this.''

Then before he even knew what he was intending to do, Durango yanked her into his arms and captured her lips with a kiss.

He experienced the kiss not just with his mouth and tongue but all the way through to the very center of his body. His gut whirled and his groin tightened and even his frickin' knees bobbled.

Abby resisted at first, pushing against his chest with the flats of her palms. But then her jaw loosened and her tongue rushed out to meet his. Her hand fluttered upward and she skimmed her cool fingertips over the heated skin of his neck.

She wanted this as much as he did. Even if she couldn't admit it.

The realization inflamed him.

Durango deepened the kiss, splaying a hand at the

small of her back, holding her steady while he poured every drop of concentration into kissing her.

God, he'd forgotten how good she tasted. How he'd once dreamed of planting himself between her supple thighs. His old dreams came roaring back to life. Twice as big, twice as potent, twice as hungry.

He was in dangerous territory and he thrilled to it, reveling in the daintiness of her slender arms, the press of her soft breasts against his hard chest.

She pulled back to catch her breath. Her eyes were wide and nervous. Quickly she glanced around.

"Durango," she gasped, and then held a palm across her mouth and nose to stifle a sneeze.

"There you go, clogging up that passion. Let your-self experience it, Abby, and you'll stop sneezing."

"I can't do that. We shouldn't do this. What if someone sees us?"

He groaned. How many times had she said that to him? How many times had he held back, respecting her wishes even though he had wanted her so badly he had thought he was going to explode from the pressure.

But they weren't kids anymore and she was on his turf now.

"To hell with what we shouldn't do," he growled, and dragged her back into his arms.

She stiffened and he could feel the conflict waging in her body. Physically she wanted him, but emotion-ally she was scared of letting herself go, terrified of embracing her sexuality.

He had honored her wishes when they were teen-agers, but not now. Not this time. He was going to make her face the situation.

Deny this, Angel.

Lowering his head, Durango captured her luscious lips again. He felt the zap of wildness flowing from the rocks, through his feet, up his body and into hers.

The feminine vortex.

They were fused into a single power source, their passion one with the cosmos. They melded with the environment. Merging, mixing, marrying the earth.

It seemed to Durango as if they were spinning from a dizzying aerial viewpoint. Their kiss captured in the Technicolor red of the soaring pinnacle cliffs and rugged desert landscape.

Overhead, a red-tailed hawk cried ''keer, keer.'' A spiny lizard skittered nearby. The air smelled of piñon pine, juniper and Abby.

In the nine years he had been guiding Jeep tours through Sedona, Durango had experienced the enigmatic power of the vortices hundreds of times. Sometimes he felt a mild tugging. At other moments it was a strong pull. Sometimes the sensation made him emotional. Sometimes he felt centered and grounded. On occasion he found himself simply overwhelmed by the vastness of the cosmos.

But never had he experienced what he was feeling now.

It was magical. Surreal. Otherworldly.

Native American lore spoke of it. This rush of incredible sensitivity. It was as if a fire hose had been turned on in his heart and he was a channel, a catalyst, a crucible.

The phenomenon was scary as hell because it felt so damned wonderful.

His body burned like a furnace. His skin tingled. Joy bubbled inside him, fizzy as mineral water.

Wow.

He let Abby go and stepped back. He could tell from the bewildered expression in her eyes that she was feeling it too.

Stunned, they simply stared at each other.

''Was that it?'' she whispered. ''Is that what the vortex feels like?''

He gulped. ''Yep. That was the vortex.''

''Oh thank heavens, for a minute there I thought that maybe...'' She didn't finish her sentence. Instead, she raised a quivering hand to tuck a lock of hair behind one ear.

He knew what she thought, because he was thinking the same thing. If simply kissing her in a vortex could cause such a euphoric sensation, what in the hell would happen if they were to make love in one?

SHE HAD TO REGAIN CONTROL of the chaotic emotions jumbling inside her. Simultaneously, Abby felt ecstasy and fear, bliss and dread. But she refused to show Durango her confusion. Her father had trained her well. Never reveal your weakness to your enemies.

And Durango was indeed her enemy, because with just one kiss he threatened to smash to smithereens her carefully ordered world.

Maybe that wouldn't be such a bad thing, whispered her high-spirited Gypsy blood. Maybe your uptight, insular world needs destroying. And hey, maybe you would quit sneezing.

Abby shook her head. She didn't know if it was the vortex or Durango or a deadly combination of both, but she would not allow herself to disintegrate over one little kiss.

One little kiss? Ha! More like the kiss of the millennium.

Knock it off. Get it together. You're Judge Archer's daughter, so act like it.

You're Cassandra's daughter, too.

Abby ignored that thought, smoothed the wrinkles from her linen shorts, squared her shoulders and glanced over at Durango.

"I think we should go check on Tess," she said evenly, and started past him for the trailhead.

Durango reached out and snagged her elbow, stopping Abby in her tracks. "I think we should talk about what just happened."

"Nothing happened."

"Dammit, don't shut me out. Not again."

"Please remove your hand." She glowered at him.

He let go and stepped back. "Are you going to be like this for the rest of your life?"

"Be like what?"

Even though his hand was gone, she could still feel the imprint of it on her skin. Already she was feeling that swoopy, looping out-of-kilter sensation in the region of her heart—she used to feel it whenever she was around him and she didn't like it.

Not one bit.

"Dead to life," he said.

"I'm not dead to life." Did he really believe that? "I just don't choose to put my feelings on parade like *some* people."

He reached up to stroke a strand of her hair. "Admit it, Angel. You're afraid of your passion. Even your nose knows it."

"Stop calling me Angel."

"Why? Because it makes you feel something?"

Yes. Precisely.

"Because I'm not that silly little seventeen-year-old who was once so infatuated with you."

"You weren't infatuated with me. If you'd really cared about me, you wouldn't have sided with your father and mine against me when you knew in your heart I shouldn't have gone to jail." His tone hardened.

Lovely. Now he was getting angry. She didn't want to fight with him. There was no point rehashing the past. They'd both made their choices.

"Don't try to put this all on me. You gave me an ultimatum, Durango, and hey, news flash, you *did* vandalize your stepmother's business."

"And you know why I did it."

"It was still wrong."

"That's the reason I started calling you Angel," he growled. "Because you're so damned perfect. You never get mad or hurt or do stupid things like the rest of us."

"I get hurt plenty. I hurt when you left town and never came back. Just because I couldn't go with you, it didn't mean I didn't want to."

They stared at each other, the past a shimmery ghost between them. Abby realized what was wrong. They'd had no closure. No true ending to the relationship that had budded hot but never bloomed.

Well then, have a fling with the man. She could just hear Cassandra egging her on. *That should give you plenty of closure. And whew! Can he kiss. Do it, Abby, do it. Mend fences.*

No. She wouldn't. She couldn't.

Why not? Too chicken? Too afraid you can't handle the likes of Durango Creed?

Argh! Why couldn't she get her mother's irreverent voice out of her head?

"We have unfinished business, you and I. That kiss said it all." Holding her gaze, he leaned in close.

"It was the vortex, remember?" She stiffened and tried to the ignore the distinct tickling sensation between her legs.

"And like I told you, the vortex gives back what you bring to it."

"What are you insinuating, Durango?" Her heart skipped a beat.

What if? What if? What if?

He reached out and cupped her cheek with his palm. His fingers were warm and strong. How easy it would be to get swept up in the past. "What I'm saying, Angel, if you're interested, is that I can show you how to unearth your passion."

Go ahead, say yes. Just have a fling and get Durango out of your system once and for all so you can get on with your life.

She gulped. She was in over her head and drowning in ebony eyes that could send a girl straight to hell.

"What precisely are you suggesting?" she whispered.

"An adventure." Durango's smile was wicked to the core. "To broaden your horizons."

She shifted her weight. She was already getting antsy, wanting to kiss him again.

Could the affair start now, please?

She wanted him so badly she was practically panting. But was this the right thing to do? What if she really was like her mother? What if, once released, there was no putting the genie back in the bottle?

"You're worried," Durango said, "that this adventure will change you in some elemental way."

"Yes."

"There's no getting around it. Once you taste the thrill of passion, you can't go back to being the way you were before."

She felt as if she were burning up and freezing all at the same time. She wanted him and yet she was terrified of losing herself, of going crazy wild. Her entire identity was tightly entwined with her father, her community and her job. How could she turn her back on all that?

"You're afraid of being ostracized from the things you care about. Of losing everything comfortable and familiar." Durango nailed her fears dead on. "The way Cassandra and I both did."

She nodded, anxiety and desire a snarled web in her throat. She hated rocking the boat. She was known for bending over backward, sacrificing her own wants and needs to keep everyone else happy. Peace at any price. That had been her motto.

"What you don't understand, Abby, is how much I gained when I left Silverton Heights."

"What did you gain?" Her heart was thumping, her breathing rangy.

He pressed his mouth against her ear and murmured, "Myself."

Abby shivered. Was this man the devil, tempting her to break all her own rules? Or was Durango actually her redeemer, offering her a chance at salvation before it was too late?

For her, it was a monumental gamble. If she made the wrong choice, her life could be destroyed.

But if you make the right one, your life could be transformed forever.

She hovered on the brink of indecision. She did not have to go through with this. She could go back home. Forget she had ever been here. Forget finding her passion. Forget Durango Creed.

The silence between them was interrupted by the sound of a cell phone ringing from inside Durango's backpack. He rummaged around in the pack, found the phone and answered it.

He looked surprised and handed it to Abby. "It's for you."

"For me?" Who could be calling her on Durango's cell phone? "Hello?" she said.

"Abby, I'm glad I caught you."

"Daddy? How did you find me here? Why are you contacting me at this number?"

She turned her back to Durango, walked a few steps away and lowered her voice. She didn't want him overhearing her conversation.

"I phoned the Tranquility Spa and they said you were on a Jeep tour. Then I called the tour place and they gave me the guide's cell number."

"What's up?" She swallowed hard. Her father would have a hernia if he knew the tour guide was Durango Creed.

"You need to come home."

"Has something bad happened?" She splayed a hand to the back of her neck.

"No, something good."

"Oh? What's that?"

"Ken's come back. He's realized what a mistake he made. It was just a case of wedding-day jitters. He wants to make things right. He wants to see you."

"He can want in one hand and wish in the other, Daddy," Abby found herself quoting one of her mother's favorite sayings. Except the word Cassandra frequently used wasn't "wish" but something much more colorful.

"Now that's not like you."

"Ken stood me up at the altar. He took off to Vegas with a stripper. I'm not taking him back."

"And he's sorry for what happened. He's begging your forgiveness."

"What'd she do? Roll him?"

"Excuse me?"

"The stripper. Did she take Ken's wallet?"

"And his Corvette," her father admitted.

"Cassandra said this would happen."

"Since when do you listen to anything your whack job of a mother has to say?"

"No name-calling, Daddy."

"You're right. I'm sorry. Just come home so we can straighten this out."

"I'm not taking him back."

"He's a good man who made a bad mistake."

"Ken's a jackass!"

"Abby," he chided. "I thought you said no name-calling."

"I changed my mind."

"All right, you don't have to marry him, but you do have to smooth things over. As the election draws nearer, you two are going to be working very closely together. We can't afford animosity to derail this team."

"You didn't fire him?"

"Honey, Ken's my campaign manager."

"And I'm your daughter!"

"Who is normally very sweet and easy to get along with and a great mediator. I know you can do this."

"You want me to swallow my pride? Tuck my tail between my legs?"

"I wouldn't ask, but you know how important the campaign is. This riff between you and Ken could negatively impact my career."

"Then fire him."

"I need him, Abby, and you know it."

More than you need me?

Disappointment had her blinking back tears. Apparently her father didn't care about her happiness or what she needed as long as his boat didn't get rocked.

All he cared about was what she meant to his precious image, his sacred campaign.

"I'm sorry, Daddy, but I just can't. I've got a lot of thinking to do. I need to find myself."

"Abigail," he commanded. "You come home right now."

"You can't order me around. I'm not seventeen anymore."

She heard her father draw in a deep breath. She could see him clenching his jaw, kneading the bridge of his nose with his forefinger and thumb, composing himself. He wasn't accustomed to her defiance. She could tell by his silence he was trying to figure out the best way to handle the situation.

"You know," he said after a long moment, "this is how it started out with your mother. Going off to find herself. It was supposed to be for a weekend, then it became a week and then she ran off with that bohemian freak who made artwork out of garbage because she had to be free to follow her passion."

"Daddy, don't make me feel rotten about this."

"Feelings are a choice, Abby. I've taught you how not to act on them."

"And now, it's long past time I learned how to express them."

Her father grunted. "Thinking back on it, I believe Cassandra was exactly your age when she went bad." He sounded bitter, resentful, and it felt as if he was lashing out at her, trying to make her feel lousy for wanting to lead her own life.

Guilt, betrayal and sadness formed a leaden lump in the center of her stomach. She had the strangest urge to eat macaroni and cheese or mashed potatoes and gravy. To bury her emotions with comfort food.

His intimidation tactics weren't going to work. Not this time. She wasn't going to cave and let him have his way.

"Cassandra isn't bad," she said, her voice cracking. "She's just a free spirit."

"Sugarcoat it all you want. Your mother abandoned us."

"I'm not abandoning you, Daddy. I just need to be by myself for a while."

"You're with Tess," he retorted. "Not by yourself. And I'm worried she's going to lead you astray."

"Daddy, please."

He heaved a heavy sigh. "All right. Take whatever time you need, just please, while you're running around getting in touch with your feelings or following your passion or whatever it is you're bent on doing, don't embarrass me. If this little escapade creates a scandal and ends up costing me votes…"

She'd never in her life hung up on her father, but she did then, switching off the phone and handing it back to Durango.

Ever since her mother left them, Abby had always taken her father's side. Cassandra was the irresponsible one. Her father had stayed behind to raise her. But Abby had a sudden inkling into her mother and for the first time she saw her parents from an adult perspective.

The dissolution of their union couldn't have been as one-sided as Abby had imagined. She realized her father wasn't as blameless as she'd always believed. It must have been very difficult for carefree, fun-loving Cassandra to make a go of marriage with a work-obsessed man as cautious and set in his ways as the judge.

"Your father?" Durango asked.

She nodded.

"He wants you to come home."

"Yes."

"Are you going?"

Abby hesitated. "No."

"What are you going to do?"

Abby shrugged. What was she going to do?

A small prop airplane buzzed overhead. She glanced up and saw it was skywriting a message. She shaded her eyes with a hand, watching as the pilot looped and twirled, forming a word of white smoke.

When the pilot finished and she saw what was etched ephemerally across the sky, her heart almost ceased beating.

There, in spotty cursive writing, was the answer she'd been searching for.

Freefall.

4

"ABBY?" Durango reached out to catch her just as her knees buckled. "Are you all right?"

"The sun, the vortex. I feel faint."

"You're probably dehydrated. Let's get your head between your knees."

He eased her to a sitting position on the ground and fumbled in his backpack for a bottle of water. He crouched beside her, handed her the water and massaged her shoulders as she drank.

Her neck muscles were a minefield of corded knots. Durango felt Abby's entire body tense at his touch and her reaction sparked a corresponding tightness inside of him. Ten years ago he had tucked her memory to the back of his brain, forgetting for the most part how much he had once wanted her.

And how much she had hurt him. A decade of censored desire came springing back and he was that horny eighteen-year-old again, starving for her body, hungering for her affection.

He didn't like feeling susceptible. He stopped rubbing her neck.

A dribble of water rolled down the curved plastic

bottle, dropped onto her upper chest and trickled slowly down the V neck of her T-shirt and disappeared between her breasts.

Durango sucked in air.

He stared at her chest.

His fingers twitched to touch her once more but he wouldn't allow himself the luxury.

He had the sudden fear that if he acted on his impulse he would be forever damned.

His mouth slipped open and he found himself tracing his tongue along his lips. He glanced at the water trickling down her breasts and looked away and looked at her again. He felt the energy of the vortex wrenching at him.

Unbelievable.

Even after all this time the woman still held the power to command his total attention. Luckily she was gazing up at the sky and hadn't noticed him ogling her. What would she say if she spotted stark need for her in his eyes?

"The skywriting," she whispered, and gestured upward. "Freefall. Like the medallion on the rearview mirror of your Jeep."

"Yes," he said, startled to find she was trembling. Apparently, he wasn't the only one waging a war with his feelings.

Her vulnerability touched him bone deep. He'd always thought of her as strong, resilient and in full control of her emotions. It was an eye opener to learn he was mistaken.

"What does it mean?" She turned to look at him.

"Freefall is a new adventure package being offered by Sunrise Tours and I'm going to be one of the guides. The itinerary will include push-yourself-to-the-limit activities like hang gliding, bungee jumping, hot-air ballooning and skydiving," Durango replied, happy to have something to think about besides the growing pressure in his groin.

"That's what you were talking about? That's the kind of adventure you meant?" Was it disappointment he heard in her voice or relief?

"What did you think I meant?"

Her cheeks reddened adorably. "I thought that… when you said that you would help me unearth my passion you meant…er…something different."

"Different how?" He wasn't going to let her off the hook. He wanted to hear her say the words. He wanted to watch her squirm.

She drew her knees to her chest, folded her arms over her head and dropped her forehead to her knees. She laughed with embarrassment. "I'm such an idiot. I thought you were talking about a sexual adventure."

I was. He just smiled and shrugged.

"So you weren't thinking about having sex with me?" Her voice was low and smoky.

If she only knew what he was thinking. She'd likely slap his face and run away.

''Angel,'' he said. ''I'm not going to lie. I would like nothing more than to take you to bed.''

''You would?''

She sounded surprised. How could she be surprised when he was practically panting? Durango felt hot, moody and restless. His mind as well as his body was burning with the fantasy of possessing her.

He knew if he hoped to seduce her that he would have to play it cagey. They had a rocky history and that was a strike against him, plus she had always been skittish when it came to expressing her sexuality.

But the kiss they had shared told him she was ready, even if she didn't yet know it. She was searching for her passion. If he played his cards right, he could possess her.

''But I'm not going to make love to you,'' Durango announced.

''You're not?'' No missing the emotion in her voice this time. She *was* disappointed.

''Not until you're ready. I won't be accused of coercing you into something you're not one-hundred percent into. Particularly when you're already mad at your dad. I don't want to be the instrument you use to get back at him. When the time comes, I want you to beg me to make you come.''

''Oh.''

She exhaled sharply and angled him a coy glance over her crossed arms propped against her knees. The sheen of desire clouded her hazel eyes. Her dark brown lashes fluttered and she moistened her lips with a saucy pink tongue.

He was incredibly aware of her. He could feel her everywhere on his skin. In his nerve endings, in his pores, hell, even the hairs on his head seemed alive with her. He'd forgotten how much she affected him.

It was disturbing.

And stimulating as hell.

"So you *would* make love to me if I asked you to?" she said.

"Are you asking?"

"Tess thinks I need to have a wild fling. She claims that's what went wrong in my relationship with Ken. That I never had the opportunity to…um…explore my fantasies before we got engaged."

"And you want me to be your guide in fantasy land?" He didn't know how he felt about this. He was good enough for a hot tryst but not good enough for a long-term relationship?

Okay, so he did know how he felt about it. Her statement pissed him off.

"I didn't say that was what I wanted. I'm just telling you what Tess thinks."

"I want to know what Abby thinks," he growled.

"Abby's not certain what she thinks. That's what she's trying to find out."

"Are you sure I'm the right guy to be discussing

this with? Don't you remember what your father always said about me?''

"That you'd take me straight to hell.'' She grinned and his anger dissipated.

"He's right about that.''

"Maybe I'm ready for a little fire and brimstone,'' she said.

"What are you suggesting?'' He arched an eyebrow and leaned close to her.

"I don't know.''

"You do know. Say it.''

She sucked in air. "Okay, I want to discover if I have Cassandra's wild passionate blood pumping through my veins. I want to find it and then I want to get over it so that it doesn't come back to haunt me. I want to stop sneezing when I have out-of-control sexual fantasies.''

"All right.''

"But it has to be discreet. My father's running for office…I can't cause a scandal or…anything that could damage his career.''

"Oh, I get it. I'm to be your secret sin. The guy you remember fondly when you're a ninety-year-old woman sitting in her rocking chair thinking back on her past.''

"Yes.'' She bit down on her bottom lip. "Does that make you mad?''

"That you want to use me for sex and then dump me?'' His gut was in turmoil and he felt a sharp poke of something rude in his heart. "Hey, at least this time I'll get sex out of the deal before I get dumped."

"You're still mad because I wouldn't run away with you."

"No. I'm not mad. That happened a long time ago. I'm just disappointed in you."

"Disappointed?"

"That you're still letting your father run your life," he said.

"That's why I'm here, Durango. I want to make a change. I just need some help. You're an old friend and I'm turning to you to help me because you're the most passionate guy I know. But if it's too much pressure on you, hey, I understand. No biggie."

"No pressure," he said. "I'm free and easy. Sure. I'll show you how to find a passion for living. For old time's sake."

"Really?" She looked happy and terrified all at the same time.

"Really." He raised his chin and gave her his most notorious grin. He'd been told on more than one occasion his grin made women go weak in the knees.

But Abby had her force field up, her shoulders primly straight, her hands clasped together in front of her. "And you agree—what happens in Sedona, stays in Sedona? We keep our affair a secret? Tess will be the only one who knows."

"Agreed," he said.

But even as he acquiesced, some small, vengeful

part of him couldn't help thinking that all he had to do was give Abby a sweet taste of all the fun she had been missing and she would shake up the judge's perfectly ordered world all on her own and he would have a front-row seat for the show.

"YEW-HOO, Abby, Durango, if you've got your pants down, put yourselves back together," Tess's voice carried to the top of the mesa.

"Good grief, what does she think we're doing? We're on a hilltop, in full view of anyone who happens by," Abby exclaimed.

Durango chuckled. "Exploring our passion?"

"Belts buckled, shirts tucked in, we're coming up," Tess said.

"We?" Abby asked

"Don't look at me." Durango shrugged. "She's your friend."

At that moment, Tess and a ruggedly handsome man who bore an uncanny resemblance to the actor Colin Cruz appeared at the trailhead. The guy had an arm slung around Tess's waist and she was leaning against his shoulder, giggling girlishly.

"I don't believe it," Abby said. "Leave her alone for twenty minutes in the wilds of nowhere and she snags a man."

"See, that's what passion will do for you," Durango teased.

"Exactly what I'm afraid of," Abby muttered. Reality was seeping in and she was already regretting being honest with him. "Stop grinning."

He didn't stop.

"Abby, Durango, meet Jackson Dauber." Tess presented the man with a flourish of her hand. "He's Colin Cruz's stunt double."

"Hello, mates," Jackson greeted them.

"Jackson is from Australia," Tess explained needlessly. "Like Mel Gibson and Russell Crowe and that crocodile guy."

"Well, I'm not as famous as those blokes, but little sheila here seems impressed." Jackson grinned at Tess and locked gazes with her. She grinned right back.

"Who wouldn't be impressed with muscles like this." Tess squeezed one of Jackson's biceps that he obligingly flexed for her. "You're a hundred times hotter than Colin Cruz."

"He's soft as a marshmallow, luv. Can't believe you've been lusting after the likes of him."

"That's before I knew about you. And I can't believe you just happened along the trail while I was sitting there wishing something interesting would happen."

"It was fate what brought me to this vortex. That's what it was. Nothing less than fate," Jackson said to Abby and Durango. "I was meant to meet Tess today."

"Fate," Abby echoed.

"Yeah. We were supposed to shoot an action sequence this morning, but at the last minute the director decided to film the pivotal love scene instead, and on a closed set," Jackson explained. "So the rest of us got the day off. Otherwise at this very moment, I'd be hurtling down a canyon in a runaway wagon instead of enjoying the sights with my new lady."

New lady!

They'd just met for crying out loud. They were moving far too fast. Abby tried to catch Tess's eye to mentally say, slow down, slow *way* down, but Tess's full attention was focused on the hunky stuntman.

"Oh, Jackson," Tess simpered, hanging off his beefy arm like a groupie.

Stunned, she stared at her friend. If she didn't know better, she would swear Tess was in love. But she couldn't be in love. How could she be in love? She didn't even know this person.

"Jackson hiked out here all the way from the movie set. Can we give him a ride back to Sedona, Durango?" Tess asked.

"Sure."

Abby shot Durango a dirty look. Why was he encouraging them? Oh yeah, right, because he was a huge proponent of passion. But from this side of the fence, the passion simmering between Tess and Jackson looked ripe for someone getting badly hurt.

And Abby feared that someone was Tess.

"Thanks, mate." Jackson slapped Durango's palm

and winked. Abby didn't like what that wink suggested. Not one bit.

"We were just heading back," Durango said.

By the time they reached the Jeep, the sun was at its zenith and several more tourists were in the area. Tess and Jackson climbed into the back seat, Durango and Abby in the front.

As they were pulling onto the road, a man slipped from behind a rock. He raised his camera, snapped their picture, and then disappeared from where he had come.

Abby recognized the guy. He was the vortex-seeking tourist in the Bermuda shorts, plaid socks and Van Halen T-shirt combo.

"That's weird," she said. "Why was he taking our picture?"

"Paparazzi," Jackson said. "They're all the time mistaking me for Colin Cruz."

"Gosh, I bet that's exciting," Tess said.

"It's a pain in the arse, is what it is."

"Hmm," Abby murmured. She couldn't say why, but she had the distinct feeling the guy wasn't paparazzi. There was something about him that didn't fit.

"Where can I drop you, Jackson?" Durango asked when they wheeled into Sedona.

"Tranquility Spa."

"You're staying there?" Tess squealed. "That's so cool. Us too."

"Now that's what I call a pleasant coincidence," Jackson said.

"It's fate is what it is." Tess leaned against his shoulder. She was already picking up his vernacular.

Oh *pull-eaze*, Abby thought, but secretly part of her was jealous at how easily Tess got swept away by her emotions. She didn't stop to analyze or strategize or compartmentalize. She simply seized the moment with both hands and reveled in life. Come what may.

No letting a little common sense and fear of pain slow her down.

When they reached the Tranquility Spa, Tess and Jackson tumbled out of the back seat and headed inside together. Durango reached over and touched Abby's arm, detaining her.

"So," he said. "About this passion thing. Are you still game? Tomorrow is my day off and I thought we could start with something really fun."

"I…I'm…I'm…"

Now that they were away from the influence of the electric vortex, Abby's bravery vanished. She was having serious second thoughts about the wild fling they had discussed out on the mesa. She wanted it, yes. But she feared it too.

"Conflicted," Durango finished her sentence for her. "Plunging into an impetuous affair isn't really your style."

"No, it's not and you're right, I am conflicted. On the one hand you're incredibly sexy and I'm looking forward to fanning that old flame. But on the other hand, I don't want to treat you shabbily.''

''Don't worry about me.'' His smile was gentle and oddly relaxing. ''I get your hesitation. You've been telling yourself for so long that you're sensible and calm and unemotional. Challenging your core values and beliefs takes a lot of courage.''

''The deal is, I'm not even sure I want to challenge them.''

''Of course, you do.'' His knowing grin was easy. ''Or you wouldn't be here with me.''

''Tess set this trip up. I had no idea she was plotting to get me to Sedona to see you again.''

''But you allowed her to make the travel arrangements,'' he said.

Abby inhaled audibly. ''I did.''

''And you know what she's like.''

''Yes.''

''I stand by my statement. Subconsciously, you want to be here.''

He had a point.

''It's not that I want to change my beliefs and values,'' she said after a moment. ''There are just some things I need to discover about myself before I can move forward with my life.''

''What exactly do you want from me, Abby?''

''I want the adventure of a lifetime,'' she said, barely able to believe she had the courage to ask for everything she needed from him. She'd spent her life trying to smooth things over, giving in to what other people wanted and rarely giving thought to what she wanted.

Until now.

It was a new and totally liberating concept, one she was going to enjoy trying on for size.

"Then that's what I'll deliver," he promised. "I'll pick you up at five o'clock tomorrow morning."

"Five o'clock?" Abby was by nature an early riser, but five in the morning?

"We're going hang gliding at dawn."

"Hang gliding?" she squeaked. "I'm not sure I need an adventure quite that intense."

"That's just for starters. It's gonna get much more intense."

"Oh?"

"Oh, yeah." Then Durango drew her into his arms right there in front of the main entrance to the Tranquility Spa.

Abby wasn't comfortable with public displays of affection, but she didn't know how to pull away without looking uptight and prudish.

"I need to take this one baby step at time."

"Angel, hang gliding is nothing," he said. "We'll be flying tandem. I'll do all the work—you just relax and enjoy the view."

"What if I can't go through with it?" she whispered. "What if we get up in the air and I panic? What if I freak out? What if I go on a sneezing jag?"

"Passion rule number one. You freak and the game is over. You're in total control."

"This goes for when we make it into the bedroom, right?"

"If we even decide to make use of a bed." His tone sent chills of anticipation coursing down her spine.

"I've never had sex anywhere but in a bed," she admitted.

He clicked his tongue. "That's what I was afraid of. Passion rule number two. No beds."

"And passion rule number three, what is it?" she whispered.

"Just let go and let it happen." He hooked an index finger under her chin, tilted her face up and then lowered his lips and kissed her right there in front of the smirking bellboys.

"Those guys," she mumbled around his lips. "They're watching us."

"Let 'em stare."

"What if they talk? Remember, if we do decide to consummate this affair it has to remain a secret."

"Let 'em gossip. This isn't Silverton Heights. No one is going to tattle to your daddy."

"I can't gamble with his career."

"So I'll pay 'em off to keep quiet."

"I'm serious. This is important."

"So are you. When are you going to stop putting everyone else's interests ahead of your own?"

"You don't understand," she started to protest, but he placed a finger over her lips.

"Shh. Concentrate on what you want and forget everything else."

She inhaled sharply.

Durango was kissing her and looking her straight in the eyes at the same time. Abby was so startled by the sheer thrill racing through her that she didn't close her eyes either.

Their gazes were locked as tightly as their lips. She'd never kissed with her eyes open and she was surprised to discover how incredibly erotic it was.

Durango pulled away. "Did that panic you?"

"A little," she admitted. "If you weren't holding my shoulders I might have run away."

"Fair enough," he said. "But it was exciting, too, wasn't it."

"Yes," she confessed.

"Liberating."

"Uh-huh."

"Just remember, Abby, you're in charge of any and all adventures we go on together. Sexual or otherwise. If at any point you get too scared to continue, we stop. Nothing happens that you don't want to happen."

"Thank you, I appreciate that."

"Unless," he said, his tone pure chocolate sin, thick and rich and gooey with innuendo, "*you* decide you want to relinquish all control and abandon to abandon."

5

ABANDON TO ABANDON.

Surrender to surrender.

Capitulate to capitulation.

Abby lay on the bed, staring up at the ceiling. All this letting go sounded tempting, but was she really cut out for adventure, excitement and pushing her sexual envelope?

More important, what if it turned out that she *was* so cut out for passion that her old life no longer fit? What if it turned out Cassandra was right?

What then?

Tess picked that moment to burst through the door of the room they were sharing, startling Abby from her daydream.

"It's official," her friend said, dramatically clutching a hand to her heart and falling backward across her bed. "I'm in serious lust."

"What else is new?" Abby asked dryly.

"I'm telling you, it's the power of the vortex. This place has made a believer of me."

"What has the electromagnetic energy of the earth got to do with lust?"

"Everything."

"Okay, if you say so." Abby shook her head. She would never have guessed Tess would fall for this crazy vortex stuff. Then again she had felt something pretty amazing on the top of the mesa.

"Seriously," Tess said earnestly. "I mean it. I haven't had the hots for anybody this badly in a long, long time."

"Bull," Abby challenged. "Yesterday you were madly in lust with Colin Cruz."

"Oh, he was just a fantasy." Tess fanned herself. "But trust me on this, Jackson is very real."

"Did you guys have sex already? Please tell me you didn't already have sex with him, Tess." Abby glanced at her watch. "You've known him all of five hours."

"We didn't have sex." Tess smiled knowingly. "Unless you call groping each other in the tranquility garden having sex."

"Just how much groping went on?"

"Let's just say the tranquility garden wasn't exactly tranquil while we were gettin' it on."

"Tess! People come to this spa to relax. Have some consideration."

"Hey, they relax their way, I relax mine."

"You're incorrigible."

"And you love me for it. Without me your life would be a total yawn fest."

"That's not fair," Abby said defensively. "I do interesting things."

"Name one."

She frowned. She worked at her job, she helped out on her father's campaign. She exercised faithfully and attended church on Sundays. For fun she piled onto the couch and watched movies in her pj's and slippers. To relax she cooked gourmet meals. For enjoyment she listened to classical music.

Okay, so Tess had a valuable point. She was unarguably dull. That's why she was embarking on this adventure thing with Durango. And to prove Cassandra wrong. She was determined to establish a precedent. She was going to show her mother that a person could indulge in passion, then walk away from it without destroying anyone's life in the process.

"Well?" Tess prodded.

"I hang out with you," Abby said at last.

"There you go. I'm your salvation. I provide your life with much-needed contrast."

"Are you seeing Jackson again?" Abby asked, anxious to switch the subject off her boringness.

"You betcha. He's sneaking me onto the movie set tomorrow and we're planning on making out in the stuntmen's trailer. Isn't that exciting?"

"Just don't get caught."

"Why not? What's the worst that can happen? I get tossed out. No big deal."

"Jackson could lose his job."

"You think?"

"Maybe."

"Oh. I hadn't thought about that. I'd hate for him to lose his job."

"See, there is a downside to the whole impulsive fun-loving thing. So settle down. Besides, you don't want to end up just another notch on his belt."

"Why not? I'm carving out a notch with his name on it on *my* belt."

Abby shook her head. "One of these days you're going to get your heart broken." She just hoped it wasn't soon.

"Not me." Tess waved a hand. "I'm the heart-breaker, not the other way around. I've learned my lesson from my parents' mistakes. There ain't no such thing as true love. It's all a Cinderella fairy tale."

"That's so cynical."

"Hey, considering what you've been through with your folks and then getting dumped by Ken I think you'd be on the love-is-bunk bandwagon yourself."

Abby shrugged. "What can I say? I have high hopes."

"And speaking of high hopes, let's dish about the delectable Mr. Creed. God, is he ever yummy. So is he the same sexy guy you remember?"

And so much more.

Abby shrugged nonchalantly. She wasn't ready to talk about her feelings for Durango. She needed time to process what had happened.

"Did you guys fool around on the mesa? That's why I hung out on the trail, to give you some alone time. That is until Jackson came along and then I sort of forgot all about you."

"Yes," Abby admitted. "We kissed."

"Well?" Tess rolled over onto her belly and propped her chin onto her stacked hands. "How was it?"

Abby tried to play it cool, but the memory of their kisses bubbled up inside her like a happy secret she just couldn't keep to herself.

"It was incredible."

"Elaborate."

"All I can say is wow."

"So is it like you remember?"

"Oh, it's so much better. When we were teenagers I was too uptight to relax and Durango was too eager to take it slow. But he has really matured. And he fills out his jeans nicely, I might add." She giggled.

"Well, so when are you seeing him again?"

Abby sobered. "He's taking me tandem hang gliding tomorrow. That is, if I don't end up backing out."

"Why on earth would you back out? This is exactly what you need."

"You know me, Tessy. I like having my feet planted firmly on the ground. This whole gliding-over-the-earth thing…" She shook her head.

"Mmm-hmm. And where has keeping your feet firmly planted on the ground gotten you so far? Working at a job you just sort of happened into. Attending a university your father picked out for you. Engaged to the dullest man this side of dirt.''

''You're making my life sound horrible and it's not. I find being connected to something bigger than myself, like our community and the charitable organization I work for brings me peace of mind. I'm not like you. I don't have to feel the earth shift every five minutes in order to feel alive.''

''Does it really bring you peace of mind?'' Tess challenged. ''Or are you just saying that because you're afraid to have sex with the dynamic Mr. Creed and find out exactly how wonderful it feels to have the earth move under your feet?''

''I'm just worried these adventures will change me and not for the better.'' Then Abby told Tess about her father's phone call.

Tess sighed. ''Don't worry. You're not going to turn into Cassandra.''

''How do you know that? Eve ate the apple and everything changed.'' Abby snapped her fingers. ''Just like that.''

''What if everything changes for the better? What if your father actually ends up approving of your bid for independence—once he gets used to the idea— and he applauds your growth?''

''I don't think that's going to happen. He was pretty upset with me. He's afraid I'm going to sabotage the election.''

"You know what you need—" Tess began.

"Oh no," Abby groaned. "That statement is what landed me in this quandary in the first place."

"Getting dumped by Ken for Racy Racine is what got you into this situation. I simply added fuel to the fire. Listen up, what you need is to change something about yourself right now."

"What have you got in mind?"

The idea intrigued her. Changing something small might give her enough courage to try something much bigger and bolder.

Like hang gliding.

And having non-bed sex with Durango.

"You could borrow my clothes. Wear something hot and sexy. Ditch those classy, tailored threads of yours. You wanna wear my turquoise tank made out of that special weave fabric that clings to your boobs like plastic wrap?"

"The one that shows off your midriff?"

"That's the one."

"Maybe," she hedged.

"You could pair it with my low-rise bell-bottoms. It makes a jaw-dropping ensemble. Especially if you wear those adorable suede half-boots of yours. You know, the ones with the chunky heel."

What could a change in wardrobe hurt? She didn't usually go in for belly-baring styles, but why not? No one in Silverton Heights would ever need to know she was prancing around Sedona with her navel on display.

"And, you've worn your hair in the same don't-muss-me style since you were a teenager," Tess mused.

"You think I should cut my hair?"

Gulp.

"The spa's salon is supposed to be world-class. Go ahead. Whack it all off. Make a bold statement. Cut it short and sassy in one of those unruly artistic styles. I think it would look fabulous."

"Isn't that kind of drastic?"

"Drastic is the key. Besides, it's just hair, Abby. It'll grow back."

Tentatively she reached up to touch her smooth, obedient shoulder-length tresses. Shearing it off would be a bold step. Was she ready for this?

If you can't even cut your hair, how can you hope to have exciting sex adventures with Durango?

"Come on. Liberate yourself." Tess made cutting motions with her fingers. "Snip, snip," she dared.

DURANGO SPRINTED into the lobby of the Tranquility resort spa at 5:06 a.m. the following morning, heading for the courtesy phone at the front desk. He sailed right past Abby before it registered who she was.

He stopped in mid-stride and slowly turned around to face her. His jaw dropped.

"Abby?"

She was standing to one side of the door, illuminated in the soft glow of ambient lighting from the chrome wall sconces. She wore the tiniest turquoise top that hugged her breasts and rib cage but went no lower. The skimpy shirt showcased her taut, amazing abdomen and perfectly shaped navel.

They had dated for almost three months when they were teens and he'd never seen her navel. Now she was giving him full view. Somehow it felt naughtier than if she'd been totally naked.

But the surprises didn't stop there. He was speechless to discover she had chopped off all her long, sleek, beautiful hair and he didn't hate it. In fact, he found the short, sexy flirty style irresistible. The sassy cut shouted *fun, fun, fun.* And the fringed, side-swept bangs emphasized both her wide hazel eyes and her full sensuous mouth.

A heady concoction of testosterone-driven adrenaline flooded his brain with a barrage of carnal images.

In a blinding flash he saw them, arms and legs entangled, their sweaty bodies lying in a panting heap, their senses raw with the taste and sound and sight of each other, their bodies throbbing and sensitive from the aftermath of diabolically great sex.

The thought of being the one to unleash her pent-up passion weakened his knees and made his heart chug sluggishly.

He was so excited by the changes in her, it was all Durango could do not to ask the desk clerk for a room, scoop Abby into his arms, storm upstairs like Rhett Butler with Scarlett O'Hara and ravish her senseless. But he'd promised her wild, unconventional sex. Besides, he wanted her as desperately hot for him as he was for her.

Until then, he would contain himself.

If he could—

"Durango?" she interrupted his fevered reverie with a timid tone in her voice.

"I...I..." he stammered, "didn't recognize you."

He'd been looking for his elegantly groomed, conformist Abby, not this rebellious, sexy imp. Self-consciously, she reached up to touch her hair. It lay flat against the nape of her neck, exposing the creamy curve of her shoulder.

"What do you think about my hair?" she asked. "It was Tess's idea."

"Never mind what I think," he said. "Here's the important question. What do you think?"

"I don't know." She was studying his face, trying to gauge his reaction. "I haven't had time to get used to it."

Durango wanted to tell her it didn't matter to him whether her hair was long or short, sleek or tousled. What made her his Angel was her ready smile, easygoing laugh and compassionate heart, but he wasn't sure she was ready to hear it.

Nor was he so sure he was ready to say it. Things were still too iffy between them.

"Yes, you do know. Abby, do you like your new haircut?" He was determined to break her of this habit of seeking everyone else's approval before forming her own opinion.

"I...well..."

"Answer the question," he growled.

"Okay, I like it. In fact, I think I love it. It's so carefree and easy and I feel ten pounds lighter and younger than I have in years."

"I like it too," he said.

"Oh, thank heavens." She exhaled and it was only then he realized she'd been holding her breath. "I was afraid you would hate it."

"Even if I did hate it, which I don't, it's your hair. Wear it however you want. Stop looking outside yourself for validation."

"Do I really do that?"

"Yes, you do."

"How do I stop?"

"Come on." He reached for her hand. "I'm going to show you."

The pulse in her neck throbbed as hard and fast as his own heartbeat, but she took his hand and let him escort her to the Jeep.

It was still dark outside and the tandem hang glider he'd borrowed from Sunrise was strapped to the roof. He helped her inside, then hurried around, got in and started the engine.

"I brought you hot chocolate and a blueberry muffin." He nodded at the sack on the seat between them.

"You remembered I drink cocoa and not coffee," she said, and he could tell from her tone of voice and the soft look in her eyes that she was touched by his gesture. "That was so thoughtful of you."

For no good reason he felt oddly embarrassed. "What can I say? You made an impression on me. They say you never forget your first love."

"I wasn't your first love," she scoffed. "You went out with lots of girls before me."

"I had girlfriends, yes, but you were the first one I went gaga over."

"You were just hot for me because I wouldn't ride on your motorcycle, or put out."

Her tone was light, teasing and, while there was some truth in her statement, his attraction went far beyond the thrill of the chase. He had remembered her in a way he hadn't remembered any of the others.

She'd been special and it wasn't simply because she'd been the one who got away. She'd intrigued him because she'd been so perfect in an untouchable way and he'd had the unrelenting urge to muss her up.

Or maybe, just maybe, it's because she was the one who broke your heart.

Abby sipped her cocoa and Durango reached over to switch on the radio. Knowing she liked classical music, he tuned it to that station.

"Why don't you put it on something hard driving," she said. "Rock or hip-hop or rap."

"Why? You don't like that stuff."

"But you do."

"Stop trying to please me."

"I'm not. I'm trying to discover what it is that I really like. It just occurred to me that I listen to classical music because that's what my father has always listened to."

"Okay." He dialed in a popular dance station that played a variety of high-energy tunes.

He shot her a surreptitious glance as he drove, still trying to get used to the hair. Had she cut it to show him she was ready to escalate their relationship?

Whoo-boy.

He hoped he hadn't bitten off more than he could chew. He had shot off his big mouth and told her he could show her how to feel passion. Now that she was sitting here next to him, he wasn't so sure. He could show her his passions, but could he help her find her own?

A jittery sensation akin to panic clenched inside him. Okay, he was panicking.

Big time.

What if he failed her? What if he couldn't shake her out of her comfort zone? What if she freaked out on the hang glider the way she'd freaked out when he had tried to take her for a ride on his Ducati? What if she decided he was too much for her?

Over the course of his twenty-eight years, he'd shared his passions with many women. Some had taken to their adventures wholeheartedly, others had tossed in the proverbial towel, unable to handle the intensity of his extreme lifestyle.

But this was different. This was Abby. Her whole future lay in his hands. If he failed her, she would go back to the life someone else had chosen for her, never having realized how huge the world was outside Silverton Heights.

No. Durango refused to let her down. Abby had come to him for help and he intended to devote himself to igniting her passion. One way or the other, he would succeed. She deserved to know the rapturous bliss just waiting for her if she learned to trust in herself and embrace her desires.

By the time they reached the launch site several miles outside of Sedona, the Jeep was throbbing with the pounding beat and the sun was peeking over the horizon.

Abby helped him unchain the hang glider from the roof of the Jeep, and ten minutes later they were standing on top of the launch slope strapped into the tandem harness together. The air was fairly chilly this time of day and she was glad she'd brought a sweater even though she figured she'd be shrugging out of it soon.

"How you doing?" Durango asked.

"Nervous."

"Nothing to be scared of. I'm right here." He squeezed her shoulder.

She clamped a death grip on the harness strap and peered over the side of the slope, trepidation causing her heart to pound.

"The plane seems so flimsy." She eyed the light metal structure.

"It's very sturdy." He rocked it for her to see that it wasn't going to fall apart in flight.

"How do you steer it?"

"I hold on to the control bar and shift my weight in relationship to the glider."

"Sounds complicated."

"It's not. But you just relax. I'll all do the work."

"Sounds a lot like sex," she joked.

"Not with me it doesn't. When we get around to the sex, I expect you to work up as much of a sweat as I do. Far as I'm concerned, you give as good as you get."

"Oookay." The expression in his eyes rattled her to the core. It was if he knew she'd never been very athletic or inspired in the bedroom.

"Does that scare you?"

"I just hope I don't disappoint."

"Don't worry," he said. "I'm a very patient man. Both in bed and out."

"What if I hate hang gliding?" she said, quickly changing the subject before she started sneezing uncontrollably.

"You just let me know and we'll land. But be fore-
warned, once we're committed to the launch, we're
committed until we're in the air."

"All right."

"But give it a chance."

"I wish I had a Valium," she muttered.

"You don't need medication. You can do this. I
have faith in you."

He knew it was the right thing to say. She hated to
disappoint anyone. She blew out her breath and
squared her shoulders. "I'll give it my best shot."

"Hey, if you can cut all your hair off, this will be
a piece of sponge cake, babe," he said, and then gave
her a short preflight briefing.

She was placing herself at his mercy, trusting him.
It was a big step for her. She couldn't believe she was
actually doing this. The woman who was once too
afraid to even ride on the back of his motorcycle was
about to jump off a cliff with flimsy wings strapped
to her back.

"The weather's perfect. There's a smooth breeze
coming up the slope. I'll just radio into Sunrise and
give them our flight plan." He called in on his two-
way radio and gave their location and landing coor-
dinates to the Sunrise dispatcher.

"Now we're ready," he said, clipping the radio to
his belt. "Helmets on."

They strapped on their helmets in unison.

Abby blew out her breath. "What next?"

"We start running down the hill. Just run as hard as you can."

"That's it?"

"That's it. Here we go. On three. One, two, three."

They took off over the edge of the cliff.

"Keep running as hard as you can until we're airborne," Durango coached. "Hang on to the harness strap and don't grab on to the control bar at any time during flight."

"Okay," she said breathlessly, legs pumping.

And then they were in the air, suspended by their harnesses, flying side by side in a prone position, the wind beneath their wings lifting them higher and higher into the sky.

Durango's shoulder grazed against hers. His body was slightly above hers and when he moved to steer the craft his hip bumped provocatively against her behind.

"Oh," Abby gasped, fascinated as much by his nearness and the brush of his body as the rush of the flight.

She was acutely aware of everything. His manly scent, the sensation of weightlessness, the vastness of the view, the intoxicating taste of freedom on her tongue.

"You all right?"

"Perfect," she whispered. "Absolutely perfect."

The glider soared over the earth, whispery as a

feather, light as foam. The silence astounded her. A hawk circled gracefully not far away.

Breathtaking scenery stretched below. Red rock canyons, enchanted buttes, antediluvian steeples regally dotted the landscape like Zen helixes transmitting primordial voltage into the atmosphere.

Abby felt it. The power. The energy. The thrill. It was a current of vitality emanating simultaneously from the earth, the air and their bodies.

She sneaked a glance over at Durango. The expression curling his lips was as awe inspiring as the spectacular vistas drifting beneath them.

The cool yellow-orange fingers of sunrise caressed his face. His eyes were alight with a rarefied glow, the smile on his mouth beatific. He was flying far beyond her, his mind kissing the heavens.

How she wanted to go there with him.

He cruised on the thermals, his full attention focused on maneuvering the glider. She could study him and he wouldn't notice. They swooped and circled, wheeled and rose. Two human birds experiencing the sky.

This then, Abby thought, watching the sunlight play across Durango's euphoric features, is what they mean by passion. He loved what he was doing. Loved flying and nature and autonomy.

Durango had passion for the sky. For adventure. For life. He had what she wanted.

Idly she wondered if this was what his face looked

like when he was having sex. Totally absorbed, bliss-
ful, engaged. That irreverent thought set her whole
body to tingling.

Abby felt a corresponding cacoëthes begin to bud
inside her. A tiny knot of something so special she
feared that if she examined the feeling too closely it
would vanish. Enough to say she felt a lightness, a
joy she had never experienced.

She savored it. Basking in the wind against her
skin, the heat of the rising sun warming her cheeks,
the birdlike sensation of skimming over the earth.

It felt like liberty and redemption rolled into one.
Up here, who could have worries or fears, dreads or
concerns?

For the moment, she was completely free.

Durango, she whispered to herself and his name
felt like a prayer. *Durango.*

"I see a good spot to land," he said, pointing at
the desert floor.

"Already?"

"We've been up over an hour. General rule of
thumb for a first flight is only twenty minutes."

"We've been up an hour? Really?"

"It's been eighty minutes," he confirmed, and
twisted his wrist around so she could see his watch.

"Wow. I would have guessed ten." She couldn't
believe it. She'd been so caught up in the flight, time
had ceased to exist. She'd been in the zone.

"Besides, we're near some ancient Indian ruins

that aren't on any tourist's map. I thought you might like to see those while we wait for the pickup crew to retrieve us.''

''Sounds interesting,'' she said, although she was reluctant to leave the sky. They couldn't keep this up forever, could they? Swooping and soaring and dancing with the clouds.

''I'm going to position myself above you,'' he said, ''as we come down.'' His voice was throaty and the way he said ''come'' and ''down'' embellished the words with thick innuendo.

''Come on down,'' she whispered, teasing him with the same suggestive tone.

She felt so light. So bold.

He put his arms on either side of her shoulders. His chest was pressed against her back. His pelvis was even with her bottom. The breeze gently rocked him into her, his zipper bouncing against the seam of her jeans.

Bump, bump, bump.

Abby's body flushed with sudden, painful need. She closed her eyes, but that was worse because she saw them flying naked, his penis slowly sliding in and out of her as they rocked in tandem.

In and out. A sweet, sensuous aerial glide.

Holy cow, she was a freakin' pervert. She shook her head and opened her eyes.

Stop it. Stop it.

Durango triggered the pneumatic wheels for landing and to bleed off the speed. The earth rushed up to greet them.

"Start running if your legs hit the ground before the wheels do," he said.

But Abby, who couldn't shake the erotic feeling of Durango's fly bumping against her butt, lost her concentration. She stumbled and fear squeezed hard, replacing her earlier euphoria. Panic-stricken, she grabbed for the control bar.

"Hands off the control bar," Durango yelled at her.

She jerked back and fell to her knees. The glider was dragging her through the dirt.

"Abby, get up," he said urgently, and reached for her.

She stuck out her hand and he glanced down to grab for it. He pulled her back up, but by the time he regained control, they were already in trouble.

"Oh shit," he said, whipping the glider around.

"What! What is it?" she cried just as her legs dipped down again and her bottom slammed into something firm and a stinging pain shot up her backside.

"Cactus!"

6

———————

DURANGO HAD TRIED his damnedest to steer out of the cactus patch but no such luck—a saguaro got Abby in the end. Literally. At least he'd managed to avoid the vicious cholla cactus.

Thank God. Those things would eat you alive.

However, Abby was getting her first taste of the downside of following one's passion.

He unclipped himself from the glider and his gear, then quickly unbuckled Abby from the harness and peeled off her helmet.

She blinked, trying hard not to give in to the pain. He knew from experience those damned cactus spines well and truly hurt.

"I'm so sorry," he apologized.

"It's not your fault." She swallowed bravely. "I'm the one who panicked and grabbed the control bar after you told me not to."

"Why did you freak?"

"I thought we were going to crash," she confessed. "It seemed to me that something so incredible was bound to end in disaster."

"You're seriously twisted, you know that?" He

shook his head. "Equating pleasure with catastrophe."

"I didn't say my fear made sense. I'm only relating what I felt."

He studied her a long moment. The woman had some screwy ideas about life. Durango had an irresistible urge to prove how misguided her beliefs were.

But he had to give her credit: she was trying. Ten years ago she would never have considered hang gliding, much less do it. His admiration for her escalated while at the same time he had to caution himself not to care too much about her. She'd cut him deeply once before, and he wasn't going to give her the opportunity to hurt him like that again.

"I have a first-aid kit," he said. "Which includes pocket pliers. Let's just get you somewhere comfortable and out of the sun so I can extract the thorns. Can you walk?"

"Uh-huh." She grimaced.

"The Indian ruins are just over that rise. It's shaded and there's a creek nearby."

"Okay, let's go."

It only took a couple of minutes to hike to the place where sycamore trees provided a broadleaf canopy beside a narrow, trickling creek. Good thing that it was still May. Any later in the year and the creek created from the spring runoff would be dried up.

Abby wasn't the outdoorsy type, but she was holding her own. Bucking up under the pressure and rising to the occasion. Durango took her hand and led her to the rocky overhang that hundreds of years before had been stone dwellings.

It was cool inside the crumbling structure. The front was gone, but there was still a semblance of a roof overhead to shelter them from the sun.

He seated himself on a large flat red rock and opened the first-aid kit. He took out the pliers, alcohol pads and a tube of antiseptic ointment.

"Come here."

She minced over to stand in front of him.

He studied the curve of her full lips and thought about how much he wanted to kiss her again.

"This is going to be uncomfortable," he said. "Taking off your jeans to get at those stickers."

She nodded. "Do what you have to do."

With him sitting and her standing, the fly of her jeans was positioned at his eye level. He reached out and undid the snap on her flap.

His fingers accidentally grazed her bare belly and it almost felt as if he'd been burned, his reaction to her was that volatile. He slid the zipper down and realized his fingers were sweating. Not from the heat, but from the tension. He couldn't have been more nervous if he'd been juggling TNT.

Gently, carefully, he began edging her pants down over her hips.

The shallow rising and falling of her belly was barely perceptible as she breathed. He tried not to notice the subtle movement, tried not to be affected by the sight of her bare flesh, but hell, he was just a man and she was some kind of woman.

He felt himself grow hard and he clenched his jaw to fight off his arousal.

Nothing doing. The boner was there to stay.

Ignore it.

Right.

"Ow," she whispered. "Ow. The needles are catching on my jeans."

"Turn around," he ordered. He hadn't meant to sound sexually commanding, it just came out that way.

Her eyes widened and then she obeyed, giving him a wondrous glimpse of her backside. She was wearing white cotton thong panties. What a soul-sizzling combination of innocence and lust those panties were.

Never mind his lust. The thong would make extraction easier and she could probably keep her panties on.

Lucky for him.

Or maybe it was unlucky.

"I'm going to pull the fabric away from your fanny," he explained.

"Okay."

Durango placed one palm flat against her lower back and used his other hand to stretch the denim material out as far as it would go and slide it down.

Once he had gotten past the thorny area, he quickly shucked her jeans to her knees.

She stepped out of her pants, resting a palm on his shoulder to balance herself, and kicked the jeans aside.

Her breathing was as raspy as his. He didn't dare look into her eyes. He had work to do. Cactus needles to extract.

"Bend over my lap," he said.

She laid herself across his knees and he almost shot his wad right then and there. Only through sheer will did he manage to retain a thread of control.

"You've got a hard-on," she whispered.

"I know."

"I'm responsible?"

"You see any other sexy, gorgeous, almost-naked woman bent over my knees?"

"No."

"Okay. Now that we've ascertained I'm a complete animal, how about we concentrate on getting those thorns out of your backside."

Her inhalation of air was jagged, shaky. "Do your thing."

Sensations, emotions, memories collided in his brain and body at warp speed. No single thought registered. Instead, he experienced a montage of pleasure, excitement, anticipation and restlessness.

How many nights had he lain awake and dreamed of holding a near-naked Abby?

A hundred? Two hundred? Whatever, it had been an agonizingly high number.

The years tumbled away and he was eighteen again, hormones raging through him, mind consumed with the steady ache of his erection, totally absorbed with lust.

He remembered necking, groping, fondling on the front porch swing of her father's house, tantalized by the notion that the judge might open the door and catch them at any time.

He recalled how excited he'd been back then. Getting so close to making love to her and being held at bay by her fears.

Durango believed that he would never again find that same intense level of sexual excitement he had experienced back then.

He was wrong.

Here was Abby, splayed across his lap, her vulnerable tush exposed to him. Her breasts, covered only by a bra and skimpy shirt, squashed against his knees.

She was everything he'd ever hoped for and so much more.

Although she was trim and lean, she wasn't skinny. She possessed subtle curves and delicate arches like a dancer. No hourglass figure but seriously sexy all the same.

She smelled of rose-scented soap and windblown sunshine. No heavy perfume, just a sweet, precise, womanly fragrance. The skin of her derriere was baby soft and delightfully pale.

Her heart was racing, fast as his own. He could feel it pounding through her chest, into his knees, spreading all throughout his body. *Lub-lub-lub-dud,* they vibrated in unison.

''Durango?'' she whispered low and throaty.

''Uh-huh?''

''Aren't you going to pull the needles out?''

''Um…yeah…just making sure I can see them all.''

''Oh.''

In the light from the cave opening, he studied her buttocks and found the angry thorns. They were in a cruel clump. Fifteen or twenty of them inflamed her flesh, causing her skin to pucker red from their irritating sting.

Gripping the pliers firmly between his thumb and fingers, Durango began to pluck.

Pluck. Pluck. Pluck.

Abby's rib cage was pressed flush against Durango's lap and she could feel his hardness straining against his jeans, poking audaciously into her side. He was embarrassed over the boner, she could tell, but Abby was not. She felt proud. Honored that the sight of her bare bottom had reduced him to this.

She grinned.

The palm of his hand was pressed flat against her

unafflicted butt cheek. From out of nowhere, she found herself wishing he would spank her.

Just a few quick swats. Lightly but firmly. She wanted to hear the sweet smacking sound, wanted to experience the erotic thrill of being gently paddled.

She closed her eyes. What was she thinking? Allowing her imagination to run wild was what had gotten her with a rear end full of cactus needles in the first place.

What was this strange passion? This unmanageable yearning to fantasize about him?

Abby shuddered. How did she get over something like this?

"Did I hurt you?" Durango's tone was thoughtful, concerned, caring but at the same time heavily laden with treacherous undercurrents.

"No, I'm fine."

"Almost done. This is the last one." He plucked out the remaining thorn. "Just let me check and see to make sure none escaped."

He trailed his hot finger over her bottom, gently probing, innocently looking for more cactus spines. But the inferno he had started inside her was anything but innocent. The building pressure was heavy and reminiscent of the way he'd made her feel when they were teenagers making out on her father's porch swing.

But this was different. This sensation was stronger, more urgent, more full-bodied than those long-ago

stirrings. Those feelings had been tinged with caution
and tempered by her youth. What rampaged through
her now was pure animal need.

"Feel any pricks?" he asked, his fingers still
strumming.

"You mean beside the one poking me in the side,"
she joked sassily. The new haircut had given her more
courage than she realized and she loved her new bravery. Loved the person she was becoming.

"I'm sorry about that, Abby..."

"Don't you dare be sorry." She spun around in his
lap, and settled her legs on either side of him. Her
knees were bent up under his armpits. Her pelvis
pressed against his erection. She dropped her arms
around his neck and stared him in the face.

"Kiss me, Durango," she commanded.

The chocolate in his dark eyes melted to syrup. His
mouth crushed hers—hungry, demanding, just the
way she wanted it. His tongue thrust past her teeth,
discerning, exploring, then teasing and savoring. His
hands massaged her breasts through her skimpy shirt
until they were sensitive and stiff.

Without warning, he lifted her off his lap and sat
her to one side. He stood up and shrugged out of his
shirt, casually letting it drop to the stone floor of the
ruins. Beneath the button-down shirt, he wore a plain
white tee. With lightning-fast fingers, he stripped the
tee over his head and flung it to the ground, too.

His muscular chest was much broader than she remembered and covered with a light carpet of springy ebony hair. Abby stretched out her hands and rubbed both palms against his nipples, feeling the strong, steady thumping of his heart.

Her raspy breathing echoed off the eroded walls of the ruins. With a soft growl, he pulled her to her feet and tugged her into his arms.

His biceps bunched as he held her. His tongue flicked out to wreak shivery havoc against her tender skin. He kissed from the hollow of her neck to the gentle swell of her breasts.

Then he kissed down her torso to her flat abdomen and, when he reached her panties, he dropped to his knees and clamped a hand around her waist to steady them both.

With the other hand, he inched her panties down and when she noticed where his eyes had fixed, saw the wonder in them as her dark brown tuft emerged.

The scent of her womanhood rose from between her legs. The deep musky aroma aroused her, the smell of her feminine power stoking her desire to even loftier heights. She was an ancient goddess in here and this man was kneeling before her in awe.

''Babe, you are gorgeous.''

He removed her panties over her feet. She stood there wearing only her belly-baring tank top and sexy little half-boots.

The smells and sensations inundated her. The outside heat of the Arizona sun versus the shaded cool of the sycamore trees. The rich aroma of sand and man. Abby was inebriated by him, his lips, his tongue, his erotic foreplay, the hint of hidden menace that turbocharged her libido.

"Lean your shoulders against the wall," Durango demanded.

She was barely breathing. He was going to take her here in the crumbling red rock ruins of the desert. Lay her down on the ancient soil and plunge his hot flesh into hers.

How primitive. How utterly erotic.

"Lean against the wall," he repeated. "And spread your legs."

She could not resist him. She pressed her heated back against the cool stone and positioned her legs shoulder's width apart, waiting for what came next.

"Good," he said. "If you need to get your balance, do what you need to do, but hang on."

"What are you intending?" She curled her toes inside her boots, eagerly anticipating his sinful purpose.

"What do you think?"

"No one has ever done that to me before."

"Not even Ken?"

"You've got to be kidding."

He laughed gleefully and covered as much of her as he could with his mouth.

What she felt at first was gratitude mingled with a touch of shame. This felt so very naughty yet so damn right. Soon, the sweet sensation of his tongue teasing her most tender flesh took away all thoughts of anything except the physical reality of what was going on inside her disorderly body.

She moaned. "Aah. Durango."

"Yes, yes, say it again," he whispered, and then went back to what he was doing.

Abby writhed hotly against him. "Durango, Durango, Durango."

"Aren't you sorry you sent me away all those years ago?"

"I was a fool," she cried, flailing blindly. "A silly, scared fool."

"This is the sweetest revenge of all," he said. "Taking you out of yourself. Changing you. Making you mine at long last."

But she wasn't his. She wanted to correct him, to make sure he understood she simply wanted to find her passion, not start a relationship with him. This was about sex and lust and excitement, not commitment. How could there be anything else between them?

He was simply her tutor. Her passion mentor. He had turned his back on her world and she didn't belong in his. Anything other than a sexual liaison was out of the question.

Before she could voice her concerns, his tongue licked away all her protests, all her common sense. She would talk to him later.

For now she was awash in pleasure and stunned to find she wasn't the least embarrassed exposing herself to him. Indeed, she felt like a flower kissed into bloom by the thermal power of the sun.

She savored the wild, sensory ride, for once ignoring her cautious side. She felt out of control and that made her edgy. It seemed he was threatening everything she held dear and yet she could not resist him. Could not turn him aside. Could not tell him to stop.

His touch was incredible and she was unprepared for her body's volatile reaction. She trembled and ached as his tongue caressed her.

She grasped his hair between her fingers and pressed her shoulders hard against the rock, tilting her pelvis upward to give him easier access to her silky treasure.

Gently his mouth manipulated her taut peak until it was stiff and throbbing.

''Oooh.'' She moaned and thrashed, tugging on his silky hair, barely able to tolerate the exquisite achiness of it all.

''That's right, moan for me, Angel.''

She clung to him, wanting so much to climax. His tongue flicked, nuzzled, teased. The slippery wet sensation was incredible. His fingers glided into her molten center and she rocked against him while his tongue and lips continued to work their magic.

The dual sensation of fingers and tongue was more

than she could take. She was tumbling, fumbling, stumbling in a cauldron of fire.

He suckled her aching hood, ever so lightly running his tongue over the straining nub.

She bucked and thrashed, moaned and whimpered. She tossed her head, a restless mare blazing to be covered by a champion stallion. She was dripping wet for him and so hot she wanted to rip off her skin.

Building, ever building to crescendo.

This was heaven, this was hell. It was maddening and incredible, infuriating and awesome.

"I can't stand it. Make me come, Durango. Make me come." Abby couldn't believe what she screamed, but it was what she wanted. Desperately.

Passionately.

What he was doing felt forbidden and raunchy and wonderful.

Her calm control was shattered, shredded into a million tiny fragments.

He was far above mortal man. He was raw strength and raw mind. He defied the decree of polite society. He made his own rules, lived life on his own terms. He was an outlaw of sorts, banned from his homeland, living in splendid exile among the red rock cliffs.

She was afire, alight, alive with need for him. She was caught in the swirl of his magnetic masculine energy. Tossed by his powerful, unrelenting current.

Her pulses kicked. She was invigorated with need

and a vicious sort of joy. So this was passion. This impetuous, absurd orgy of the senses.

At the last moment she tried to push him away, tried desperately to reclaim her equanimity because she couldn't stand one minute more of the torturous bliss. If she allowed him to make her come, Abby suddenly felt as if she would pitch headlong into a bottomless abyss with no hope of salvation.

The fear was too unsettling and as soon as the thought entered her head, she started sneezing.

"It's too much." She sneezed. "Please, please, it's too…too…*aachoo*."

He stopped, pulled back and looked up into her face. "Do you want me to quit?"

"Yes." And then her throbbing, achy body changed her mind. "No."

And then just as quickly as the sneezing had come upon her, it disappeared.

"Don't stop," she begged, and pushed his head against her pelvis, shocked by her wanton actions but thrilled by them too. She was jerked in opposing directions. Passion on one side, caution on the other.

The same old crossroads that had always defined her life.

Abruptly Durango jerked away. "No. This isn't right," he said. He rose to his feet but did not meet her questioning gaze. "No matter how much I might want to make love to you right now, I can't."

"Wh…what?" She blinked.

He was rejecting her? Her passion-addled mind wasn't functioning properly. She didn't understand what he was saying, why he was pulling the plug on their sex play.

"Why not? I want you to."

"I'm doing it for all the wrong reasons."

"What reasons?"

Before he could answer, the two-way radio at his belt crackled.

"Come in, Durango," the smoky voice of an older woman broadcast loudly in the confines of the ruins. "Buster and I found the glider, cowboy, but where are you?"

GRATEFUL FOR Connie's timely interruption, Durango mentally chastised himself all the way back to Sedona. He was disturbed over the red-hot desire that burned so intensely whenever he was around Abby.

In the beginning, he had to confess he had wanted revenge for the way she'd once treated him. But his dishonorable bid for retribution was backfiring.

Big time.

He had lost control. He was getting ensnared in a trap of his own orchestration. How had he let a little emergency first-aid turn into a full-blown sexcapade?

Durango sat in the back seat of the Jeep feeling broody and moody in a way he hadn't felt since he'd lived in Silverton Heights. Abby was riding up front with Connie and they were chattering away like old friends. Connie's pedigree German shepherd, Buster, sat wedged between them. Occasionally, Abby would lean over to scratch behind Buster's ears.

Damn, but he wished she were stroking him.

That's just terrific, Creed, you're jealous of a friggin' dog.

What was the matter with him? He was officially losing his grip.

He had never intended to give Abby oral pleasure at the Indian ruins and his uncontrollable impulses had him questioning his objectives. He had promised Abby he would help her explore her passion so that she could get her erotic fantasies out of her system and return to her regular life refreshed and restored and happy. But after what had happened in the ruins, he was afraid that simply unlocking her secret passion wasn't going to be enough for him.

No, Durango wanted to fill her so full of zeal and enthusiasm and crazy delight that there would be no way she could go back to her hidebound life in her snooty community, where suppressing emotions and denying feelings reigned supreme. He wanted not only to rock her world, but to stand it on its head. He wanted her to see everything differently.

Especially him.

He was no longer satisfied being either her short-term stud or the bad-boy fantasy from her youth. It wasn't enough for him to possess her body. He no longer wanted to simply piss off Judge Archer.

He wanted more.

So very much more.

And he intended on having her. Mind, body, soul and heart.

He studied her reflection in the side-view mirror. Even though she was smiling and talking animatedly to Connie, there was a tension about her mouth, a famished look in her eyes, a haunted air in the way she held her shoulders.

She was not sated. She had sipped from passion's cup and she'd loved the taste.

Good thing he hadn't brought her to orgasm yet. Her hunger gave him the upper hand. She'd let down her guard and he'd slipped right in under her radar, burrowing deep inside her.

He smiled a nefarious smile.

Durango's head whirled wildly with a thousand illicit fantasies as his mind wandered down a treacherous path. He was going to bring her to her knees. Fix it so after two weeks with him she'd be unable to settle in Silverton Heights again.

He felt as if he was hovering on the verge of something epic. His portentous thoughts left him jittery and restless and eager to plot her downfall. Things were about to change.

For her. For him. Forever.

7

ABBY'S FANNY STILL STUNG from the cactus needles, but what distracted her more was the throbbing ache between her thighs. She was wild with wanting and she couldn't wait to have more adventures with Durango.

He had told her to meet him at the Conga Club at eight o'clock and to play along with whatever adventures he had in store.

As she was getting ready for the date, a knock sounded on the door. She opened it to find a delivery boy with a large white box clutched in his hands. She tipped the guy and then carried the box to the bed. With trembling fingers she pried open the lid.

Excitement jackhammered her heart. She pushed back the tissue paper and stared down at the black miniskirt, matching black zippered vest and thigh-high leather stiletto boots.

Omigod.

She clamped a hand over her mouth. It was the sexiest gift anyone had ever given her.

Inside was a card that read: *Wear me, but leave off your bra.*

She giggled but then her stomach tightened and she got scared. Could she actually wear this wild ensemble out in public? What if someone saw her? What if someone recognized her and told her father she was dancing around Sedona dressed like a dominatrix?

Abby sneezed.

No. None of that. She'd already discovered the way to get past the sneezing was simply to give in to temptation and express herself.

Here goes nothing.

She stripped off her bathrobe and put on the outfit.

The soft supple leather clung to every curve she possessed. The low-cut vest exposed far more cleavage than she was used to showing and there would be no bending over in the miniskirt, unless she wanted to moon everyone within eyeshot.

Holy cow, she looked like one sexy motorcycle chic. She wondered then if Durango still had his Ducati and if they would be riding on it.

Her nerves zigzagged every which way.

Don't back down now. This is what you wanted, remember? Fun, adventure, the freedom to be someone totally different, if only for a couple of weeks.

Both Tess and Cassandra had been absolutely correct. An outrageous, temporary fling with Durango Creed was indeed what she needed. This morning in the Indian ruins had been proof enough of that.

So, she wasn't going to overthink things. She was going to fly on gut instinct and let nature take its course and when it was time to go home, she would don her old clothes and set back to her regular life fully divested of unbridled lust, with only her sassy haircut as a reminder.

That was what she wanted.

A second knock sounded at the door.

Durango?

Could it be him? Her pulse kicked. But she was supposed to be meeting him at the Conga Club.

Unless he'd decided to change the rules.

She wobbled to the door, unaccustomed to wearing four-inch spike heels. Too bad Tess was off with Jackson Dauber. Abby could use some stiletto walking lessons.

It was the same delivery guy. But this time he was staring at Abby as if she'd stepped from the pages of his favorite naughty magazine. His mouth was literally hanging open as he handed her a vase of flowers.

She tipped him again, shut the door and set the flowers on the bureau.

Roses. Blood-crimson. A dozen.

And in the middle, one lone anthurium, a red heart-shaped flower with a gold pistil that looked like a miniature fully erect penis jutting proudly from the center.

The card read: *Does this remind you of anything?*

Abby had to wriggle her nose to keep from sneezing.

The only way to fight off the sneezes is to give in to your desires, not deny them.

Determined to conquer her quirk once and for all, Abby reached out to stroke the tiny pistil and the urge to sneeze immediately disappeared.

By the time the third knock on the door sounded, she couldn't wait to see what Durango had sent. He was spoiling her something sinful and she was loving every minute of it. She ripped open the door, took the box from the delivery guy and sent him smiling on his way with a twenty-dollar bill.

Godiva Chocolates.

The card said: *Eat me.*

So she did, savoring the chocolate like it was her last meal. Who knew Durango could be such a romantic? He was pulling out all the stops, making this the ultimate sexual adventure. He was making her feel like a fairy-tale princess, pampered and spoiled, offering up gifts to her womanhood.

She was wetter than she'd ever been in her entire life. She couldn't wait to get to him and properly thank him for his gifts.

Abby hurried downstairs, acutely aware of the stares from the other spa patrons as she passed through the lobby. The doorman had the hotel courtesy car brought around and a driver took her to the Conga Club.

By the time she arrived at the trendy nightspot, her blood was flowing lava, her heart was thumping and she was ready for action. The pounding bass of the salsa beat vibrated the sidewalk and revved her engine higher.

Abby sauntered into the club on a Godiva chocolate and romance adrenaline rush, reveling in the passion surging through her body, shoving her through the door and headlong into the throng.

Once inside, she hesitated. Many men were staring at her. Several even made suggestive comments. She felt her bravery ebbing.

And then she saw Durango.

He came through the crowd toward her.

Looking exactly as he did in her midnight fantasies. He wore a black leather vest that matched her own, except his wasn't zipped up and, as he walked, she got tantalizing glimpses of his muscular bare chest. He was powerful, almost foreboding.

Biker boy gone bad.

His leather pants were skintight, hugging his narrow hips and broad thighs. His hair, unbound, flowed sexily to his shoulders. He looked like an Indian brave on the hunt. Coming to claim his mate.

Abby practically drooled.

Even in her wildest imagination she could not have dredged up anything this hot.

Their gazes slammed into each other, a full-impact, head-on collision.

He drilled her with his eyes. It felt as if he could

see straight through her. See down, down, down into the very depths of her soul.

His chest rose and fell in jagged spikes. She wasn't surprised to realize she'd picked up his pattern and they were breathing in a syncopated rhythm.

He reached her and then, without a word, extended his hand.

She took it.

His grasp was firm, inviting. She was sucked in.

Walking backward, Durango guided Abby out onto the dance floor. Miraculously, the dancing crowd parted around them.

He moved his hips with a mind-boggling swivel, leading her to the middle of the dance floor. She had no idea he was so light on his feet. They'd both been raised attending high-society functions. They both knew the ins and outs of ballroom dance, but these wild, gyrating steps were all new to her.

Durango locked eyes with her and jerked his pelvis seductively.

Come.

Helpless, Abby felt herself drawn in. She mimicked his movements, swishing her hips, bobbing her shoulders and shaking her feet.

He stared at her but never spoke. It would have been difficult to hear him anyway over the pounding primal beat. His black eyes were enigmatic, his mysterious silence erotic. He raked his gaze over the outfit he'd bought for her to wear. His eyes glazed with a lustful gleam and his jaw tightened.

Her fingers curled with a savage urge to explore that masculine chin. She yearned to press her tongue against it, to taste the saltiness of his skin.

Durango pinned her with his eyes. They danced without ever dropping their gazes. They moved in perfect union, their bodies jammed closely together, stepping in time to the spicy music.

The other dancers were watching them, moving over, making room for the couple dressed in identical black leather. They must create a compelling sight, Abby realized, and that knowledge only served to jettison her desire into the stratosphere.

Their passion for each other escalated with each throbbing beat. They touched, skin against skin, leather against leather, skin against leather.

The band struck up the Lambada. The forbidden dance of love. The tune was faster, hotter, racier.

Durango pulled her flush against his sweaty chest. His muscles rippled against the brush of her breasts. Abby realized she was perspiring, too.

Around them other couples wriggled and writhed. Booties bounced, bottoms bumped, the smell of rampant lust was in the air. And she and Durango were at the center of it.

Their passion for each other escalated with each swagger of their hips, with every strutting dance move, dragging them deeper and deeper into a vortex of physical desire.

When the song ended, Durango leaned over, pressed his mouth to her ear and whispered, "Go to the bathroom and take your panties off."

She gasped in shock as her blood shot straight to her groin. "What?"

"You heard me."

"But my skirt is so short."

"Take off your panties," he repeated.

"I...I'm..."

"It's all part of the game," he assured her. "Just sex play. Let go of the rules."

Then he kissed her. It was a hard, crushing kiss that left no question as to what he was feeling for her. Abruptly he released her.

"Okay." She nodded, the taste of him ripe on her tongue.

She understood what he was saying. She didn't have to do anything she didn't want to do, but he hoped she would loosen up and give his game a try.

Yes. She wanted to do this. To see where it would lead. To see exactly what he had in mind.

Knees quivering, Abby hurried to the restroom. She slipped into a stall, took off her panties and stuffed them into her purse.

On her way out, she caught a glimpse of herself in the mirror and literally did not recognize the woman she saw reflected there.

Large hazel eyes made even bigger by too much mascara, short tousled hair, cheeks blushing scarlet, body decked out in decadent leather, lips swollen and reddened from the heated pressure of Durango's kiss.

A sex goddess.

A passionate überbabe.

One red-hot fox.

Salacious descriptions she would never have applied to herself before.

So this is what it feels like to be Cassandra.

That thought almost put the kibosh on her ardor and she even sneezed, but then Abby realized it was a glorious sensation. She felt emancipated, vibrant and alive.

The woman in the mirror was a bold vixen, a passion hound, a wicked femme fatale. She was the kind of woman men bought leather outfits and naughty flowers and sinful chocolates for.

This wild woman did not wear underwear.

Tonight she wasn't straitlaced Abby Archer, worrying about what the neighbors would think. Tonight, she was a rowdy sex nymph ready, willing and eager to take a big juicy bite out of life.

Emboldened, Abby stepped into the hallway.

Durango captured her from behind. He snaked a hand around her waist, murmured huskily, ''Don't you dare make a sound'' and then tugged her into a darkened alcove separated from the dance-floor area by a thick black velvet curtain. Her stiletto heels snagged on the carpet. It felt as if she were being kidnapped by a sexy bandito.

Anticipation skipped through her.

He unbuckled his black leather studded belt and yanked it fast from the loops. It made a slithering sound that raised the hairs on her forearms. He wrapped the belt around her waist and then used it to pull her hard against his chest for a long, slow, moist deep kiss.

Hadn't she once read somewhere that there was a direct connection between how a man kissed and the way he performed in the bedroom?

Good kissers make good lovers, Cassandra had always claimed.

Abby's heart fluttered. If that was true, she was in for one hell of a fine treat.

Inch by excruciating inch, Durango slid the thick leather strap down the curve of her back, until finally he had slipped it all the way to her upper thighs.

He flipped the belt beneath her miniskirt and edged it up until the leather was lying flat against her naked buttocks. Then he cocked his knee and used it to spread her legs wide.

Abby thought she just might pass out, she was that hot, that turned-on.

He cinched the ends of the belt around the bend of his knee, the belt cupped against her bare bottom. Durango's knee was stabbed ruthlessly to the wall between her thighs and she was straddling his leg like it was a pony.

"What are you doing?" she whispered.

"We are going to have our own private dance in here," he said.

They swayed with the music. His leather-clad knee was snugged against her bare bush, Abby gently riding him.

"That's it, Angel," he murmured, and bumped against her with his knee. "I want the delicious scent of you all over me."

Abby moaned and her nipples tightened to rock hard pebbles beneath her leather vest. The sensation was incredible. Now she knew why he'd told her not to wear a bra.

"That's it. Do what feels good."

He wove his fingers through her hair and held her in place while he ran his hot wet tongue up and down the length of her throat. That's when it first occurred to her that he had donned leather gloves while she'd been in the bathroom.

Totally erotic and just the teeniest bit scary. If she didn't know and trust him like she did, Abby would have been concerned.

She shivered and flexed her thigh muscles around his leg.

He stroked her collarbone with the butter-smooth leather glove. What a mind-blowing caress, this kiss of leather.

Just a single panel of curtain blocked their illicit activities from the rest of the club. At any moment, anyone could pull back the curtain and discover them.

Dragging his gloved fingers over her flesh, he increased the tension when he ran his thumb over her mouth and she detected the overwhelmingly sensual aroma of leather.

Abby moaned and arched her back as she wriggled against his leg, the pressure inside her swelling to a fever pitch.

The curtain rippled, blown by the air-conditioning. Were they about to be discovered?

What a rush.

Without a word, Durango dropped his knee and the belt fell to the floor. He grabbed her by the waist and turned her around so that her bottom was nestled against his crotch. He leaned over her to whisper into her ear, his chest pressed against her back.

"Is this what you want, Angel? Is this the kind of sexual adventure you're looking for?"

"Yes," she whimpered. "Yes."

"Spread your legs wider."

She did, balancing precariously on her stilettos while he pushed her skirt up to bare her naked buttocks.

He kept one arm wrapped around her waist, holding her steady while he kneaded her cheeks with his leather glove, then inched his hand lower and slipped his fingers between her legs.

He playfully swatted her bottom and she hissed in a breath.

"Do you like that?" he asked.

"Yes, yes."

He lightly swatted her once more, his leather glove providing erotic padding. The pressure in her feminine core twisted hard and she whimpered. She wanted his cock inside her.

Now.

"You have such a beautiful ass." He sighed and there was such rhapsody, such reverence in his voice that Abby's heart crashed inside her rib cage.

She hoped he wasn't expecting anything more from her than sex and adventure. This interlude in Sedona was going to be just that. She would cut loose, enjoy a binge on the devil's playground, then return to her life a better person for having gotten this passion nonsense out of her system.

The last thing in this world she wanted to do was to hurt Durango again.

But damn, he was an unselfish lover, thinking only of arousing her by any means possible, letting her excitement fuel his own.

Slowly he dipped one gentle finger inside her, her nectar soaking the tip of his glove. He placed the end of his pinkie over her throbbing nub with only a hint of pressure and then softly slid it off.

The slick friction, the slight force, the exquisite burst of sensation as the leather strummed her clit had

Abby's head spinning dizzily. She could not absorb it all. She splayed her palms against the wall in front of her to keep from losing her balance.

He did it again. Faster, firm. Again and again. His concentration was a thing of amazing beauty, the way he was making love to her magically electric. She felt cared for, special.

And that disturbed her almost as much as it pleased her.

Each soft snap of leather shoved her closer and closer to the edge of insanity. His fingers manipulated her, controlled her. He alternated between flicking her straining hood with his pinkie and pushing his middle finger deeper inside her.

He increased the tempo and she grew even wetter.

They were getting down and dirty. And the fact that at any moment, any second, someone might push aside that curtain and see him pressing his leather-clad pelvis against her bare bottom made her certifiably insane with desire.

More, more, more.

Through the leather of his pants she could feel the rock-hard outline of his penis. Knowing how much he wanted her only made her want him more.

His fingers pumped her. Faster, faster, faster.

Inside the sexy haze, inside the heat of her own skin, Abby squeezed her eyes tightly closed and listened to the thumping piston of her heart and the thick ebb and flow of her blood rolling through her arms and legs.

He was loving her body with his hand. Pushing her to places she'd never been, giving her new dreams to dream, fresh wings.

Pleasure lit her nerve endings; delight flooded her brain, wanting blinded her.

Lost. She was lost and could not see.

But he offered the way, his fingers promising a joy beyond anything she'd ever known.

Come.

The beat from the music throbbed through her. She was surrounded in sensation.

Leather, velvet, sweet air cooling her sizzling skin. She thrashed her head, crazy with longing, mad with lust.

"Yes," Durango whispered roughly, his voice a rasp against her ears. "Yes. Give in, surrender, let go. Passion is yours. Don't deny it."

He pressed firmly on her clit one last time and she was lost.

Abby felt heavy all over in a languid way, suspended in time, hung on the hook of the moment, impaled on ecstasy. Her thoughts were weighted, indolent. They trickled through her head like pellets slipping through the narrow neck of an hourglass, dripping one by one.

He. She. Music. Sex.

She didn't even think in sentences, just word by word. One by one.

Heat. Skin. Lips.

Life. Passion. Pounding drums.

Durango. Durango. Durango.

There was no escaping the pleasurable sensations. She was trapped. A prisoner of passion. A slave to her own treacherous desires.

She exploded.

Her body burst into the most amazing orgasm she'd ever experienced. The music beyond the velvet curtain reached a crescendo at the same time she did, drowning out her cries of pleasure.

Horns trumpeted. Drums banged. Guitars blared. Abby cried out Durango's name.

And came down hard in his arms.

8

RUBBER LEGGED and jittery with pent-up testosterone, Durango held Abby in the crook of one arm while he gently tugged her skirt back down over her bare bottom.

He had reduced her to rubble.

Was that satisfied vengeance he tasted on the back of his throat? He had corrupted Judge Archer's daughter. He was getting even with her by using her sexuality against her.

The flavor of revenge was sweet as ice wine on his tongue. Reprisal rolled down his throat warm and racy, but the aftertaste was supremely bitter. Suddenly Durango felt as if he'd eaten poisonous fruit.

This wasn't right. He should never have started this seduction.

But he couldn't turn back now. He was hooked. Addicted. Jonesing for her real bad. Right or wrong, he had to have her.

It wasn't about vengeance anymore. Or helping Abby unearth her passion. She was proving too quick a study for that.

Somehow, without even meaning to, she'd turned the tables on him and he was the one falling.

Abby's breathing was raspy in the small confines of the alcove. She was trembling and her trembling grounded him in reality.

The look she gave him vanquished his guilt. He hadn't hurt her, in fact just the opposite. She was hungry and eager for more of his tutelage.

That's when he realized Abby was his redemption and not the other way around.

He had mistakenly thought that by leading her to adventure she would discover the passionate woman who'd always been prowling beneath the cool surface. Instead, he was finding out she was taming him, drawing him back to the place he'd left behind all those years ago, making him want again to belong.

Swallowing hard, he clenched his jaw. How had this happened? Why did he have an almost overpowering urge to mend fences with everyone in Silverton Heights so he could go back home and claim Abby for his very own?

He stared at her, trying to figure out how in the hell she'd caused this change in him.

Suddenly shy, she glanced away, unable to hold his stare.

He saw her bafflement in the way she ducked her head. Heard it in the soft sneeze that shook his heart.

Durango pulled a packet of travel tissue from his vest pocket, peeled one off and handed it to her. He'd bought the tissues that morning, knowing full well that pushing Abby beyond what she'd ever experienced could induce sneezes.

But he wasn't going to stop pushing her. This was what she needed. What they both needed to close the past and open the way for a new future.

But what exactly did that future entail? She'd made it clear enough he was nothing more than a fling, a way for her to stretch her wings and clear her head.

But that wasn't enough for him. He wanted more. He wanted it all.

At that moment he knew the answer. If he hoped to win her heart he had to break her completely away from Silverton Heights. The minute she agreed to give up Phoenix and move to Sedona for him, that was when he could give up Sedona for her.

And the only way to break her was to push her to the very limits of her passion.

"I...I..." She dabbed delicately at her nose with the tissue.

"Shh," Durango murmured, and kissed her cheek. Excitement coursed though him at the thought of what was in store.

He took off the leather gloves that smelled so seductively of her and tucked them in his hip pocket. He had the sudden urge to always keep them close. He would never forget what had happened behind the black velvet curtain in the secret alcove at the Conga Club.

She was looking at him now, surreptitiously, in the dimness.

Abby worked in public relations and he could see her mental wheels turning. She was trying to find a way to put a spin on this sexual adventure that would allow her to relinquish her embarrassment.

He understood her conflict. She wanted what he had to offer, but she feared what would happen afterward. He had to show her the risk was worth the gamble.

Durango wasn't going to allow her one more second of vacillating or second-guessing. The time for action had arrived.

"No regrets allowed," he said, and then clasped her hand in his, moved aside the velvet curtain and led her back into the main part of the dance club.

The joint was hopping.

From the enthusiastic band playing the mambo to the clutch of lively dancers wriggling in the ambient lighting to the rich vibrant colors on the wall, the place screamed sex. It was why he'd chosen the location, but now he wished they were somewhere quieter, more private instead of at the most popular hot spot in Sedona.

"Look," Abby said. "It's Tess and Jackson."

Indeed, her friend and the stuntman were seated at the bar downing shots of some wicked-looking brew.

"Let's go say hello." Durango escorted her through the crowd.

"Hey, mate!" Jackson spied Durango and raised a hand. "We're having shots of Goldschläger. Pull up a stool and join us."

"Can't," Durango explained. "Designated driver."

"How 'bout you, love?" Jackson eyed Abby. "Wanna jolt? Tess is trying to get me drunk but I refuse to cooperate."

"Ain't that the truth," Tess said sarcastically.

Uh-oh, trouble in paradise? Abby glanced from Tess to Jackson and back again. There was some kind of tension between them. Sexual chemistry was surging all around, but it seemed as if they'd just had an argument or were about to have one.

"I'm a Chardonnay person," Abby said.

"It's cinnamon schnapps," Tess cajoled. "I know you like cinnamon. Go on. Try something different. Live a little. Since Jackson won't cut loose with me, I'm in need of a drinking buddy."

Abby shot Durango a glance to see what he thought of her downing the schnapps.

"Abandon to abandon," he challenged.

"Here," Jackson said, pushing the shot glass toward Abby. "Have mine."

Tentatively Abby picked up the glass and stared at the thick liqueur. "There are gold flecks of something in here."

"Twenty-four-carat gold," Jackson said, and

grinned affectionately at Tess. "No cheap stuff for my lady."

Were those two fighting or not? It was hard reading their signals. But it wasn't as if Abby wasn't getting a few mixed messages herself from the enigmatic Mr. Creed.

She wrinkled her nose. "Real gold? Is it safe to drink?"

"Much as any drinkin' is safe," Jackson joked. "Down home, they call it liquid sex."

"Liquid sex? Why's that?"

"Try it and you'll see."

Abby sniffed at the liqueur. It smelled strongly of cinnamon. She definitely needed something to take the edge off of her nervousness. Maybe this strange gold-flecked sex potion was exactly the ticket to set her free and give back to Durango as good as he'd dished out to her in that darkened alcove.

The first taste of the cordial was sharp on her tongue, almost as if it were carbonated, and very sweet. It tasted like her favorite tin of cinnamon mints.

"Down the hatch." Durango winked.

"Are you trying to get me drunk?" She met his dark-eyed gaze. "It's supposed to sex me up. Sure you can handle that?"

He leaned close. "Angel," he whispered. "If you get any more sexed up I'm gonna need a stamina transplant to keep up with you."

Her heart thumped.

She had never considered herself particularly sexy. In fact, quite the opposite. But Durango was looking at her as if she was the most sexed-up sex goddess who had ever walked the face of the earth.

Encouraged by the admiring expression in his eyes, Abby downed the rest of the schnapps, hoping it would give her the courage she lacked to ask for what she needed.

Ho-boy.

Immediately, she experienced a cozy flush in the dead center of her chest that was warmer than sunshine and twice as nice. The lush feeling curled deeper within, settling all the way to the bottom of her stomach. She felt snuggly, lovable. It was the liqueur equivalent of putting on a pair of socks hot out of the dryer on an icy-cold morning.

Yum. Cinnamon-a-licious.

Then a second wave of sensation washed over her. So much for the toasty, homey feeling. It vanished, leaving her ramped up, wired and ready to party.

She licked her lips and studied Durango. He was talking to Jackson and didn't realize she was sizing him up as if he was a juicy steak. She had a desperate urge to tie him down and lick his body from head to toe.

He was, she decided, the most doable man in the room. In fact, she couldn't wait to get out of here so they could go someplace private and finish what he'd started. She hadn't had nearly enough.

"What are you guys doing tonight?" Durango asked Jackson.

"Tess and I are just hanging out, killing time until that paparazzi bloke gives up and leaves."

"Paparazzi?" Abby asked. Her voice hummed in her ears, sweet and mellow.

"Yeah. That bloke from Cathedral Rock was hanging outside the club when we got here. Tess went to check a minute ago and he's still sitting in a white, late-model Monte Carlo in the parking lot."

"Come on, baby," Tess coaxed. "Let's dance. That cinnamon schnapps has me revved up and I want to show you how well I can shake my booty."

Jackson eyed the booty in question. "I've seen you shaking it, luv."

"If you don't dance with me, I'll have to find someone who will," she threatened.

"Well, I can't let that happen, now can I," Jackson said, and took her out onto the dance floor.

Abby watched them for a minute. They danced close, eyes locked, totally engaged with each other, but it seemed as if Tess wanted a wilder night on the town than Jackson wanted to give her.

Durango turned to Abby. "You ready to get out of here?"

"I thought you'd never ask."

"Getting bolder every day, Ms. Archer."

"Thanks to you." Their gazes clicked and the way his eyes crinkled warmed her far more than the gold-flecked liqueur.

"I've got my bike out front. You still scared of the Ducati?"

A week ago she would have been terrified, but tonight, fortified with the afteraffects of the most taboo orgasm she'd ever had and the potent heat of liquid sex, Abby was ready to chuck caution to the wind. She'd gone hang gliding this morning for heaven's sake. What was the big deal about riding on the back of a motorcycle?

"I'm up for it," she declared before she had time to think it through.

He put his arm around her waist and they left the club. They wound through the parking lot toward his motorcycle and passed the white Monte Carlo.

"Look," Abby said. "Jackson's paparazzi."

She caught the eye of the balding man in the driver's seat. He appeared startled, then quickly glanced away.

She thought his behavior was odd, but she was feeling so dreamy and amicable she didn't comment. They reached the Ducati and Durango unlocked his helmet from the handle bars and strapped it around her chin. It was too big and kept slipping down over her eyes.

"You look adorable," he said.

"Rats, I wanted to look like a badass biker babe."

"In that leather, you already do." He wriggled his eyebrows and made her laugh.

"Hey, if I'm wearing your helmet, what are you gonna wear?"

"I'll go alfresco."

"What if we have a wreck? I'd hate for something to damage that handsome noggin of yours."

"Stop worrying." He straddled the bike and held out his hand to help her swing on behind him.

It was only after she spread her thighs and wrapped her arms around his waist that she remembered her panties were in her purse. The smooth leather molded like melted butter against her *bare* muff.

You had to give her credit. When she went bad, she did it in a big way.

Just like Cassandra.

That thought dulled the afterglow of the Goldschläger. No, she wasn't like Cassandra. She was having a good time, yes. She was exploring her sexuality, opening her heart to passion, but she wasn't going to let it dominate her life.

This was a one-time fling. That was the whole point of the affair. To prove she could do it and then walk away. When she went home everything would be normal. She was in full control.

She knew she was imagining things, but she could have sworn she heard Cassandra laughing uproariously.

Durango rumbled the Ducati from the parking lot, motor thrumming.

The streets were dimly lit. Sedona had no public streetlamps and the moon looked eerie shrouded in black clouds. It was kind of thrilling, zipping around in the darkness, knowing something dangerous could be skulking in the shadows around the next corner. Abby squeezed Durango's waist tightly and allowed herself to be carried away by sensation.

She felt exhilarated. Liberated. Free.

The wind rushed over her skin, raising goose bumps of pleasure. The pulsing engine between her legs felt like a living thing. Vibrating, strumming, sending a tingling heat throbbing up through her bottom and into her spine. Her fingers, laced across Durango's rib cage, could make out every tight muscle in his honed six-pack.

The Ducati was a sexy machine. Fast and strong. She'd never been on the back of a motorcycle, had no idea it felt so impossibly licentious.

By holding herself back, she'd missed out on so much. How had she gone for so long denying her needs, doing what everyone expected of her, never questioning the status quo? She was a little old for teenage rebellion, but that's what she was doing.

And loving every minute of her newfound sense of adventure.

They left the main drag and turned off on a side

street and Abby realized she had no idea where they were headed.

Headlights came up behind them, following too close. The glare was distracting.

"I wish this guy would get off my tail. Hang on. I'm going to try and outdistance him," Durango shouted over the engine noise.

He sped up.

The scenery, from what she could see of it, whizzed by distractingly fast. The increased speed alarmed her. Abby clung to him and tried to tamp down images of being thrown from the bike.

The car sped up, too, and that's when Abby started to get scared.

"What's with this jackass?" Durango threw out the rhetorical question. "I'm going to make a sharp right turn."

She couldn't see where they were going. Abby prayed that Durango could. When he whipped the bike to the right, it looked as if they were plunging straight down the canyon.

But there was a road, albeit an incredibly narrow dirt lane barely wide enough for a full-sized vehicle.

And damn if the car didn't make the turn right along with them.

Coincidence? Or were they being followed?

Durango kicked the speed higher. He zigged and zagged, weaving over the road. Uneasiness knifed through Abby and she hugged on for dear life.

The darkness thickened the farther they traveled away from town. The Ducati's headlight cut a thin swath of illumination through the midnight black. The mesas loomed like eerie stone monsters, rising up in the very near distance.

They hit a low spot in the road and the motorcycle shimmied.

Abby gasped.

The car behind kept on coming.

Her pulse thudded, surging blood through her neck, her fingers, even her toes—encased inside those killer stiletto boots—pounded.

Her entire body rattled with adrenaline.

The car revved and edged to their left.

"I think the dude is trying to pass," Abby yelled to Durango.

"Or run us off the road," he replied with a grim expression.

"But why?"

"Drunk, crazy, who knows."

"Try slowing down, please," she begged.

The strange exhilarating bouncing inside her confused Abby. She was elated by the adrenaline rush, but also she was terrified they would crash and she would end up flying over the handlebars or Durango would crack his skull wide open.

She could see the shocking headlines. *Gubernatorial Candidate's Pantyless Daughter Injured In Freak Motorcycle Accident.*

Daddy would kill her.

"Stop, please," she urged him again, the fear of humiliation outweighing her thirst for adventure.

Durango hesitated and a weird little voice in Abby's head whispered, *He wants to cause a scandal. Why else would he make you take your panties off and then finger you to orgasm in the club?*

But then she realized how ridiculous that sounded. She dug her fingers into his ribs, letting him know just how scared she was. He'd told her anytime she said the word he would pull the plug on their adventures.

Finally he eased off the throttle.

But it was too late. Neither of them saw whatever had suddenly jumped out into the middle of the darkened road. Swerving, they did see the large rock looming before them.

The front tire hit hard.

Durango fought for control and lost. The motorcycle spun away, tossing them onto the dirt. Abby bounced on her butt. She heard the heel of her stiletto boot snap off. Her right arm scraped a rock. Instantly her elbow burned, but luckily the aftereffects of the schnapps dulled the pain.

Durango cursed fiercely.

The car shot around them.

Abby turned her head to see what kind of daredevil lunatic had been snapping at their bumper.

It was the white Monte Carlo from the Conga Club.

Durango was on his feet and calling frantically. "Abby, Abby, are you all right?"

"Fine. I'm fine."

He pulled her to a standing position and that's when she realized he was breathing as hard as she was. He'd been damned scared, too, whether he was willing to admit it or not.

They stared at the taillights disappearing off into the distance.

"That was Jackson's Van Halen T-shirt wearing paparazzi jerk." Abby exhaled.

"Obviously, Jackson Dauber is not the one he's following."

"The paparazzi has been tracking us? But why?"

"Not us, Angel. You."

"Me?" Abby splayed a hand across her chest. "Why would anyone be following me?"

"Your father is running for governor," Durango pointed out. "You're a good-girl socialite, I'm a bad-boy black sheep. Quite the sexy scandal. It would make for great gossip fodder."

"But why did the guy try to run us off the road?"

"Maybe he didn't. Maybe he just didn't want us to get away because he couldn't see well without any streetlamps. After accidentally causing us to run off the road, he panics and splits. Paparazzi are known for their brazenness, not their brains."

"That's assuming he is paparazzi."

"What else would he be?"

"Maybe he's someone my father hired to scare me away from you."

Durango stared at her. He knew Judge Archer was not above doing whatever it took to protect his only child, but to have his daughter shadowed? That was pretty low. "You think?"

"He's afraid I'm going to do something to damage his credibility. The way Cassandra did. When she left him for that garbage artist twice his age, it created a lot of ripples in Silverton Heights. He was still a lawyer back then and he lost several influential clients."

"See that's exactly the kind of thing I hate about Silverton Heights. The judgmental hypocrisy is stunningly cruel."

"You're right," she said, and her agreement caught him off guard. "And I'm really just beginning to see your side of things. You were the community scapegoat and I chose to go along with the crowd instead of believing in you. I'm sorry, Durango. I really am."

Her apology went a long way in repairing the old hurt. He shrugged nonchalantly as if it had never bothered him, but the guilt was back, needling him for his underhanded motives in pursuing a seduction with her.

"Don't worry about it. That was a long time ago."

"Yes, and this apology is long overdue."

"There's no need to apologize to me." He reached out to touch her elbow.

"Ouch!" She drew back from his touch and his hand came away sticky with her blood.

"You're hurt," he said, his heart in his throat. All his lusty plans for the rest of the evening came to an immediate halt.

"I just skinned my elbow," she said, not looking him in the eye. "My heel broke off too."

She sounded so forlorn he yearned to scoop her into his arms and just squeeze her tight. But she held herself aloof as if she wanted him to keep his distance. Durango decided to focus on checking out the Ducati.

The bike was okay. He righted it, swung his leg over the seat and glanced back at Abby. "You up to riding?"

She hobbled over and he helped her get on.

"I live just over the next rise," he said. "I could take you home with me, doctor those wounds."

He knew taking her to his house was ripe with temptation, but her elbow did need attention and he didn't want to take her back to her hotel just yet.

"I see a theme forming here. I get hurt on our adventures, you patch me up."

"That's the thing about adventures, Angel, you do get hurt occasionally."

She smiled at him then and his soul warmed. "At least I have you to kiss away my aches and make them all better."

They went to his place and Durango parked the

Ducati under the carport. He helped Abby up the front walk and into the house.

She looked around, taking it in. He suddenly saw the place from her point of view. It was totally masculine. Decorated in a rugged, outdoorsy theme, but overall he was a tidy guy.

He might toss his work gear on the table, kick off his boots by the door, but he made sure the dishes were washed and the floor was swept. He also made his bed every morning and kept the bathtub scrubbed just in case he had female visitors.

After his mom had died, Durango was the one who took care of cooking and cleaning. Until his father had married Meredith and she hired a housekeeper.

He watched Abby checking out his bulletin board where he pinned messages, notes and his work schedule. He had also tacked up a picture of himself and the group of six teens he'd taken rock climbing last summer as part of the Outward-Bound program where he volunteered.

Call it ego, but he had also posted the article his friend Eric Provost had written about him in *Arizona* magazine last winter. Eric was another disillusioned alumni of the school of Judge Archer.

In fact, that's where he and Eric had met. In jail. Durango for vandalizing his stepmother's warehouse, Eric for shoplifting diabetic test strips for his grandmother who couldn't afford to buy medical supplies.

Eric had even mentioned Durango's short stint in

jail in the article and commented on the injustice perpetrated by Judge Archer against him. Eric was making a point, illustrating how Durango had rehabilitated himself and was now helping disaffected youngsters who found themselves on a similarly treacherous path.

"Have a seat," Durango told Abby. "I'll go get some equipment to fix up your arm."

She was making him nervous, checking out his private stuff. It wasn't that he had anything to hide, but he was uncomfortable letting her know too much about himself. He wanted her to trust him, but he wasn't really ready to trust her.

Not yet.

"There's soda and beer in the fridge," he called over his shoulder and ducked into the bathroom for antiseptic and bandages.

He came back out and immediately dropped the hydrogen peroxide. It bounced twice and rolled under the table. His jaw hit the floor.

Abby was standing buck naked in the middle of his kitchen.

"Wh...what," he croaked, "are you doing?"

"I don't care about my stupid elbow," she said. "I want you to make love to me. Right now."

Well, hell, this was a wild turn of events. Durango wanted to make love to her more than anything in the world, but he also wanted to be in control of when and where it happened.

His eyes toggled from her face to her amazing body. Breasts, butt, thighs.

He longed to eat her up. He had to close his eyes to keep from caving in.

"Abby." He swallowed. "Please put your clothes back on."

"Don't you want me, Durango?"

He opened one eye. She looked completely guileless and hurt.

"Angel, I want you so much my teeth hurt. But you're skinned up, under the influence of Goldschläger and I've got another early-morning adventure planned for us. Besides, I think you're doing this for the wrong reason."

"Lusting after your hot bod is the wrong reason?" She boldly walked across the kitchen and fingered the zipper on his leather vest. "I want to feel you inside of me, Durango. I want you now."

"No, what you want is to strike back at your father for sending that guy to spy on you." He had to clench his fists at his sides to keep from dragging her off to his bedroom.

From the look on her face, he could tell he'd hit the nail on the head, but she'd been well schooled in cloaking her emotions. Quickly she rearranged her features.

He had to get her covered up, and not in that sexy leather outfit, before all his resistance crumbled and he made love to her.

Lori Wilde   157

Dashing into his bedroom, he jerked open the drawers, found a T-shirt and sweatpants.

"Here," he said, hurrying back to the kitchen to give her the clothes. "Put these on and then we'll take care of that elbow."

She tugged the T-shirt down over her head and slipped on the sweatpants. Even though they were way too big on her they'd do the job. She looked like a kid playing dress-up.

He led her to a chair, sat her down and turned his attention to her skinned arm. He cleaned and dressed the wound.

"Thank you," she told him.

Durango let out his breath, and it was only then that he realized he'd been holding it the entire time he'd been treating her elbow.

"It's after midnight," he said, "time to get you back to the Tranquility Spa."

"Can I stay here for the night?" Abby asked. "I don't want to be alone. Besides, Tess might bring Jackson back to the room."

"They looked like they were spoiling for a fight to me. I'm betting they don't consummate their relationship."

"All the more reason for me to stay. Tess will be in a foul mood if Jackson doesn't put out. The woman wants what she wants when she wants it."

"I don't have a guest room and the couch is hellaciously uncomfortable," Durango said, grasping at straws.

"I could share your bed," she suggested. "And I promise no hanky-panky. I remember your no-bed sex rule."

Okay, maybe she could keep her promises and remember the rules, but could he?

9

FALLING ASLEEP next to Durango was much more difficult than Abby imagined it would be. There was something intimate and sort of permanent about sharing a bed together. Especially when you weren't having sex in said bed and the man you'd been having red-hot sex fantasies about for years and years was snuggled up right next to you.

She closed her eyes, but she could still hear his steady breathing. His rhythm was so relaxing, she soon found herself synchronized with him, their chests rising and falling in tandem. Two as one.

Stop it. Knock off thinking like this. The deal you have going with Durango isn't about romance but sex. Remember that. Sex.

She drifted. Her body felt detached from her head. Her legs were leaden weights, affixed to the mattress, but her mind floated free, racing with a thousand dangerous thoughts.

Durango was spooned into the curve of her body, his front pressed against her back. He had settled in that position once he'd fallen asleep. Abby wished he would move, but she wasn't about to wake him up to ask him to shuffle over.

To distract herself, she thought about the man in the Monte Carlo. Had her father really hired him to spy on her and report back about her activities? He'd done it before. When she was in college and he was afraid she was dating someone he didn't approve of. Her father had also hired private investigators to check on Cassandra over the years, whenever she changed jobs or men, before he would allow Abby to visit her.

The private eyes had never turned up anything more damning than the fact Cassandra was living her life with zeal, not giving a fig what anyone thought of her. Abby used to think Cassandra was hedonistic, irresponsible and lacked self-control.

But now she saw that she'd simply adopted her father's opinion. She was finally beginning to appreciate her mother. Cassandra was romantic, exciting and fun. She valued different things than most people in Silverton Heights. That didn't make her bad. Just different.

Abby realized she wanted to be different, too. She'd started down that path the minute she'd asked Durango to teach her how to find her heart's passion.

She was loving his lessons and she had no intention of stopping, scandals be damned. Let the gossip rags write about her. Let her father find out she was indeed her mother's daughter. She was going to shake Silverton Heights to the core. She didn't know what Durango had in store for her, but she was determined to plunge into it with all the fervor she could muster.

Durango was an extraordinary man who was breathing new life into her lonely body. He had awakened her slumbering soul.

And now, it was payback time.

DURANGO AWOKE Abby before dawn with a kiss on the cheek and a mug of hot chocolate.

She came awake slowly, yawning and stretching so sexily he had to force himself not to crawl into the bed beside her.

Today promised to be magic. He was yanking off the brakes, determined to show her the true meaning of letting go.

And passion.

He dropped her off at the Tranquility Spa so she could shower and change clothes. She came back out to the Jeep twenty minutes later dressed in shorts so teeny he knew she must have borrowed them from outrageous Tess and a little halter top that caused his groin to tighten.

What exactly was she up to?

It was all he could do to keep his eyes on the road as they drove to where his launch crew waited, ready to inflate the hot-air balloon on his command.

They arrived at the site just as the sun lost its cover. ''A hot-air balloon ride!'' Abby squealed.

"Do you like the idea?" Anything that could make her that happy made him instantly happy.

"I love it." She beamed. "Flying in a hot-air balloon has always been a secret dream of mine."

He leaned over and gently pinched her forearm. "You're not dreaming, Angel. This is for real."

And so is the way I feel about you.

Durango parked the Jeep and Abby hurried over to watch the ground crew set up. Not long afterward, the balloon was ready to go, complete with a picnic basket one of his crew members had picked up for him.

He helped Abby into the woven wicker basket. The glow on her face set his heart knocking. He loved that he'd brought a smile to her face.

Above their heads, a pilot light kept the huge flame burning that heated the air inside the envelope.

When they were ready, Durango gave the signal and his crew removed the tether lines. Gently the balloon began to ascend.

Airborne, they floated on the wind.

The launch crew became the chase crew. They hopped in their vehicle and took off for the main road as the balloon climbed higher.

Abby laughed, a low, rich sound that overflowed his heart with joy.

He draped an arm over her shoulder and she snuggled against his chest and smiled over at him.

"This is incredible," she whispered.

"I'm glad I've pleased you."

"Just wait," she said cryptically. "It's my turn to please you."

He wanted to tell her that she pleased him simply by being on the planet but that would have been too much, too soon. Instead, he concentrated on stoking the fire higher, heating the air, sending the balloon higher and higher into the sky.

When he reached the altitude that suited him, he broke into the picnic basket and fished out egg-and-ham crescent-roll sandwiches and made mimosas from orange juice and champagne.

"This is so romantic," Abby said when he raised his champagne flute to hers for a toast.

"I'm glad you like."

"Who wouldn't?"

Their eyes met. "To passion," he said, and clinked his glass to hers.

"To passion."

They drank.

When they'd finished, Durango returned the used supplies to the picnic basket. The balloon had descended while they'd eaten and he fueled the hot flame higher again. It made a loud whooshing noise as the balloon rose.

Abby was gazing out over the mesas and Durango stood behind her, watching her watch the scenery. He'd brought a few women up for picnics but none of them had ever stirred him the way she did. No woman had ever even come close.

He studied the nape of her neck, exposed so fetchingly by her new short hairdo and her skimpy purple halter top. He couldn't resist. Stepping forward, he kissed that lovely, beckoning nape.

''What are you up to?'' she asked with interest as he nibbled her neck, smooth and fiery hot from the champagne, the overhead flame and the heat of his mouth.

She turned, clasped his shoulders in her hands and with newfound candor that suited her well, she earnestly fitted her moist, willing mouth against his.

It was as if they were kissing for the very first time. All heat and thrill and tentative exploration. Something was different about her. Something had changed last night.

But what?

And why?

Confused, Durango pulled back and stared into her eyes.

''We're sinking again,'' she said.

''Huh?'' He blinked, his mind numb with want and confusion.

She gestured upward.

''Oh yeah.'' He filled the balloon with more hot air.

Abby stepped to the edge again. ''Up here, in the peace and quiet, drifting on the currents, it's like we're the only two people in the entire world.''

''There's the chase crew.'' He pointed out the orange Sunrise Tours Jeep cruising the road far below them.

"It looks like a toy. We're so alone up here."

He grinned. "Yeah, I guess we are. Why? What do you have in mind?"

"First take us as high as we can go." Abby nodded at the sky. "So we'll have lots of uninterrupted time to drift down."

They rose up and up and up. He took the balloon as high as he dared. When he turned around, he discovered Abby was kneeling on the floor of the wicker gondola.

"What are you up to?" he asked, intrigued and excited.

"Face me, brace yourself against the edge of the basket and keep your legs apart."

He obeyed, his gut churning with anticipation. The balloon bobbled against his movements. They sailed along on the smooth current, riding effortless among the clouds.

Abby reached for the fly of his jeans. Durango hissed in air as she slowly slid the zipper down.

He'd been ready for this for ten years. His cock was granite hard and came jutting out of his open fly without any enticement.

"You're not wearing underwear." She giggled with delight.

"I go commando."

Lightly she stroked his head. "You're so big and

thick,'' she whispered in awe and gripped his shaft in her hand. ''I'm going to love having you inside me, filling me up.''

He just groaned.

''I'll teach you to bring me to orgasm in a semi-private club,'' she said, and then blew a stream of warm breath on the throbbing head.

He grit his teeth. A tiny droplet of his male essence leaked out. It glistened in the light. Gently she rubbed it away with the pad of her thumb.

A low, ferocious growl escaped his lips. There were so many things he wanted to tell her. How beautiful she was, how she made his heart thunder, how he'd eagerly give up everything he owned to have her.

But the words clogged his throat and he couldn't speak. His brain was addled with the intense pleasure of her mouth coming down on him.

Abby smiled to herself. He hadn't put up the least bit of resistance. Good. Very good. Let him see what she'd felt last night when he rubbed his gloved fingers around her hot, straining nub and sent her flying off into orbit.

In the beginning, she only placed her palms on his thighs and then lowered her head between his legs. She moved her face from side to side feeling the tickling velvet of his burgeoning shaft.

Then, she slipped her hands around his buttocks and tugged him toward her open, willing lips.

He filled her mouth. He swelled bigger, bigger and bigger still.

She moved her mouth around him, sliding back and forth, away and toward, away and toward.

Time stopped as she surrendered herself over to the most primal of life's rhythms.

His breathing was raspy, punctuated only by the sound of the pilot light. He was coiled tight, his entire body tensed. The muscles in the tops of his thighs seemed carved from marble beneath her palms.

He made deep, guttural noises and she knew she was pleasing him, giving him the same sweet bliss he had given her.

His erection expanded, growing harder, fuller, stretching the skin to bursting. The tip engorged with blood and pulsed hot against her lips. Abby feared she was hurting him and she eased back.

"No." He choked out the word, his fingers threading through her hair. "Don't stop."

His knees quivered. His hands shook. His trembling spoke of the deepest sensory delight.

In that moment, he belonged totally to her. Abby had never felt so empowered.

His fingers moved from her hair to her cheeks, his touch like the glide of air, like the wings of a bird. He threw back his head, let out a cry to the sky. It startled her and pleased her all at the same time.

His orgasm shook through him, an earthquake of

release, and he spilled into Abby's welcoming mouth, hot and metallic.

Give it to me, she thought. *I want all of you.*

Abby swallowed, delicately licked her lips and buried her face against him, while the sound of her pulse rushed loudly in her ears.

Durango sank to his knees beside her, gasping.

"That was...you are...I love..." he panted.

What? Was Durango about to tell her that he loved her? Panic flooded her. She didn't want to hear this. It was one thing to have an illicit affair with a thrill seeker; it was quite another to be in love with one.

"I love what you did to me," he finished.

Relief flooded her body at the same time she felt an odd sense of loss. What in the hell was the matter with her? Did she want him to be in love with her or not?

Not.

Unless...

Unless what?

He looked into her eyes, brushed his fingers over her cheek. She tucked her insecurities to the back of her mind and smiled at him. He kissed her forehead, her nose, her lips. Then he pulled her into his arms and held her tight as they drifted together, far above the earth.

ABSENTMINDEDLY, Durango guided a Jeep tour of elderly tourists out to the Chapel of the Holy Cross, his mind stuck on Abby. No matter how hard he tried to focus on his memorized spiel, he kept stumbling over words he knew by heart. He simply could not get his thoughts off what had happened earlier in the hot-air balloon.

Or the way he'd almost slipped and told her that he loved her.

Durango winced. It was much too soon to tell her what he was feeling. He didn't want to scare her off before his seduction was complete.

And what plans he had up his sleeve.

When he'd dropped her off at the Tranquility Spa, he'd stared into her eyes, stroked a finger along her collarbone and whispered, "Tonight, Angel, prepare to have your world rocked."

Durango turned down Highway 179 and didn't even realize the retired schoolteacher in the passenger seat beside him had asked a question, until she pointedly cleared her throat.

Sheepishly he had to ask her to repeat her question. Truth of the matter, he'd been thinking about Abby's skin, how soft it was, like velvet and silk all rolled into one. He was remembering how her moist, hot mouth felt on his erection, the excited spark of passion in her eyes when she'd unzipped his fly and gotten her first good look at him.

He thought about the way she reacted to his touch. How he dissolved into a pool of quivering speechlessness at the slightest brush of her hand. Erotically, she'd manipulated him, making him feel like a king among men. Appealingly, she had surrendered all restraint and swallowed his essence.

His hand trembled in remembrance.

Abby had been radiant in her feminine glow and giddy with newfound power in her sexuality. He didn't know where she had found the courage to express herself so vividly. He could only hope he was the catalyst for her growth, because she made him feel like the sexiest man in the world.

Tonight. Tonight. He could barely wait for tonight. It seemed a thousand years away instead of hours.

Tonight, he was taking Abby up to the Satan's Bridge vortex and there, he was going to make her forget herself. Forget everything.

And then tomorrow, he'd supply her with the ultimate adventure guaranteed to stoke anyone's passion to the next level.

A tandem skydive. Just the two of them, freefalling through space together.

He parked in the lower lot of the Chapel of the Holy Cross and helped his geriatric contingency out of the Jeep. He escorted them up the steep walkway and into the small triangle-shaped church built by Frank Lloyd Wright. While they visited the chapel, he went back to the Jeep to wait for them.

Slipping his sunglasses on, he leaned back in the seat.

"Durango?"

He jumped, sat up straight and ripped off his sunglasses. There was Tess, standing beside his door looking forlorn.

"Hi," she said. "Can I sit with you for a while?"

"Sure, go ahead."

She crawled up in the passenger seat beside him.

His pulse quickened at the thought of seeing Abby, and he glanced around the parking lot. "Where's Abby?"

"At the spa getting her aura read or something." Tess waved a hand and sighed deeply. "I needed to get away and think."

"What's the matter?"

Tess groaned and dropped her face in her hands. "It's not your problem."

"Why don't you try me?" he asked sympathetically. It was the first time he'd ever seen Tess looking anything but sassy and on top of the world. "Maybe I can help."

"It's Jackson."

He waited for her to continue, but when she didn't, he nudged her gently. "What about Jackson?"

"I can't get him to make love to me."

"Maybe he's thinking you're too special to rush things with."

"Ha. Yeah, right, what guy turns down a willing woman?"

"A guy who just wants to take things slow."

Tess shook her head. "Oh no."

"What?"

"There's only one reason a guy would want to take things slow."

"Why is that?"

"Because he's falling in love with me."

"Would that be so bad?"

"It would be horrible."

"All right, maybe he's not falling in love with you," Durango said, searching for the right words to soothe her. "Maybe he just doesn't want to hurt you."

"He's falling in love with me, I just know it." She wrung her hands. "He *can't* fall in love with me."

"Why not?" Durango was confused. "I thought you liked him."

"I do like him, but I don't *do* love."

"Why don't you 'do' love?"

"I don't believe in it," she said staunchly.

"Why not?"

"It's just too good to be true."

"So you're a cynic."

"Come on, tell the truth, you're not cynical about love?" Tess cocked her head.

"Hell no."

"Hmm. That surprises me. I would have thought after everything that happened between you and Abby you'd be as down on love as I am."

"Not the case. In fact, I'm a big believer in second chances."

"I wish I could be so optimistic," Tess sighed. "But life has shown me otherwise."

Durango wondered why she wasn't discussing this with Abby. It seemed like the sort of thing best friends would dissect at length. "So what happened?"

"I had too much to drink last night. I was sort of nervous because I really like Jackson and I'm afraid I don't measure up to all those cute, sexy groupies he's used to."

"You underestimate yourself, Tess."

She wrinkled her forehead. "That's exactly what Jackson said."

"So what happened?"

"Anyway, he takes me back to the Tranquility Spa, I invite him to my room. He comes in and then get this, he gives me an aspirin, makes me drink a gallon of water, tucks me into bed, kisses me on the forehead and leaves. I guess he just wasn't interested."

"If he wasn't interested he wouldn't have bothered taking care of you when you were drunk. And maybe he's just not the kind of guy who takes advantage of a woman who's had a little too much to drink."

"Okay then, I need your point of view…as a male. How do I get him to take advantage of me?"

"I think you might be pushing too hard."

"What do you mean?"

"Try dialing it down a notch," Durango suggested.

"Give the guy a chance to make the first move if he wants to."

Tess considered his advice. "All right," she said. "I'm willing to give it a try. Is this how Abby managed to snag your attention? With her cool reserve?"

Durango smiled. "Among other things." Like the way her cool reserve hide a cauldron of seethingly hot emotional depth.

"But I'm scared. What if Jackson *is* falling in love with me? I just want sex from him. Not happily-ever-after."

"How can you be so sure? Maybe if you let yourself, you could love him too."

That brought her up short. Tess paused and then said, "Both my parents have been married and divorced several times. Abby's parents' marriage was a nightmare. Give me one good reason why I should take a chance on getting my heart ripped up."

"Tess, even if things don't work out, love is sometimes still worth the risk."

She gazed at him for a long moment and then sucked in a deep breath. "Omigod, you're in love with her, aren't you."

He couldn't deny it. Ruefully he nodded.

"Does Abby know?"

"I'm trying to find a way to tell her."

"See," Tess challenged. "You might talk a good game, but you're scared too! Because you know that if she broke your heart once, there's no guarantee she won't break it again."

10

"I'VE NEVER SEEN anyone with such a red aura," Inga, the Tranquility Spa aura specialist said to Abby as she photographed her with some odd-looking camera equipment. "Actually, your aura is more than just plain red. Literally, you're flaming scarlet."

"What does that mean?" Abby frowned. Sounded like a lot of bunk to her.

"The redness comes from the base chakra. It represents the physical emotions. Anger, passion, excitement."

"Is that bad?"

"If you're searching for tranquility, it can be disruptive."

"But what if you're not looking for tranquility?" Abby asked. "What if you like being wickedly red-hot?"

"Ah," Inga said, "I understand. You are new in love with a very earthy man."

Abby shook her head. "No, not in love."

"The aura does not lie."

"It's more like lust. You know that crazy, illogical, gotta-have-him-or-I'll-die sensation."

Inga nodded. "Much trouble."

"But I can change my aura, can't I? Just because I'm red right this minute doesn't mean I'll always be swept away by passion."

"Of course you can change it. In fact, I can clean your aura right now, help you get rid of your primal feelings."

"No!" She'd worked too hard to find her passion. She wasn't about to let some New Age aura cleaner sweep away all her hard work.

"You're headed for a lot of emotional pain if you don't tone down the red. You're out of balance. Too much emphasis on the physical body."

Well heck, she already knew that, but this was a once-in-a-lifetime thing. So what if she crashed and burned. When she got back to Silverton Heights her aura could go all green or blue or purply or whatever color represented peace and tranquility. For the first time in her life, she was fully embracing her base, animal nature and she wasn't going to apologize for it.

Abby thanked the woman, paid for her session and went back to her room to wait for Tess. They were supposed to go watch Jackson on the set of his movie.

Not fifteen minutes later, a knock sounded on the door.

Durango. Her heart leaped. She knew he was working, but she couldn't help thinking maybe he'd swung by on his break. She was still thinking about what she'd done to him in the hot-air balloon. Abby grinned. No wonder her aura was flaming scarlet.

She flung open the door. Disappointment sent her smile switching from genuine to perfunctory when she saw it was Jackson.

"Hi," she said. "Tess isn't here."

"I came to see you," he said.

"Me?"

"May I come in? I need to talk to you about Tess?"

"Oh, yes, well sure." Abby stood aside and let Jackson into the room. Hands clutched behind his back, he started pacing.

"You want to sit down?"

He shook his head. "Too keyed up."

"Aren't you supposed to be shooting today."

"I got sent home."

"Why?"

"I couldn't concentrate. Kept making mistakes."

"What's wrong?"

He looked at her balefully. "Tess and I had a huge fight last night."

Abby had been worried about their romance from the start, but Jackson looked so woebegone she felt sorry for him.

"What happened?"

"She broke up with me because I wouldn't sleep with her."

"Pardon?"

"It's not that I don't want to sleep with her." Jackson clutched his hair in despair. "In fact, I want her so much I can't even think straight. But she's important to me and I don't want to rush things. I have a history of moving too fast with women and then when they get serious, I run away. But Tess is different. She's special."

"I know." Abby nodded.

"I didn't want to screw things up with her."

"Did you tell her all this?"

"Yes."

"And?"

"She said she doesn't 'do' commitment. It was either sex or nothing. What in the hell is that supposed to mean?"

"She's scared."

Jackson laughed ruefully. "Of course she's scared. I'm scared, too. I've never felt this way about anyone. But I'm more scared of losing her."

Abby reached out to touch his shoulder. "I think maybe she's falling in love with you, too, and that's why she got so panicky."

"But how do I convince her to take a chance on me, on us?"

"You've got your work cut out for you. Her childhood was a mess. She got shuffled from her mother to her father to boarding schools and back again. She's got more than a dozen stepbrothers and sisters. She can't keep them all straight. She hasn't had much of a role model for commitment. Her life's been a swinging door with people coming and going.''

"My mum and dad have been married for forty years,'' Jackson mused.

"So why haven't you settled down?''

He shrugged. "Wanted to have a bit of fun. That's what being a stuntman in the movies was supposed to be all about. But I'm thirty now. My bones aren't what they used to be and as for the girls and the parties, I've been there and done that. It's time for more and Tess is the one I want it with.''

"I respect you for that.''

"Seems you've known Tess longer and better than anyone else. Tell me how to court her.''

"Pull out all the grand gestures in your arsenal. Do something totally romantic. Let her see you mean this. Let her know sex isn't enough for you.''

"What if she turns me down?''

"Don't give up. She needs a forceful guy who can hang in there when she tries to chase you off—and she will.''

"Anything else?''

"Be there for her. Don't let her gruffness scare you. She doesn't mean it. She's just testing you. She needs to know you won't ditch her at the first sign of conflict. You're ahead of the game, you've got your mom and dad as road maps. Use them.''

"Thank you, Abby,'' Jackson said, and leaned over

to kiss her on the cheek. ''I'm going to win her heart, just wait and see.''

''Good luck.'' Abby smiled and watched him head out the door. For the sake of Tess's future happiness, she could only pray that Jackson Dauber was half the man she thought he was.

RESTLESS AFTER Jackson's visit, Abby went for a walk in the spa's garden. She'd had a facial, a massage, gotten both a manicure and a pedicure and she was fed up with being pampered. It was only four o'clock in the afternoon and Durango wouldn't be by to pick her up for hours and hours.

She couldn't stop herself from wondering what he had in store for tonight. Surely, this time they would finally be going all the way, fully consummating their affair.

But just not in a bed.

Abby grinned. Where would their assignation take place? They'd already fooled around in ancient ruins, in a salsa club and in a hot-air balloon. What could possibly top that?

Making love in a vortex.

She shivered. Yes. That's what she wanted. To feel the power of the earth's energy combine with their own cosmic kind.

Already she was getting warm at the prospect.

Feeling decidedly untranquil, she and her flaming-scarlet aura left the garden. She walked through the lobby where the desk clerk had the television turned on.

She wouldn't even have noticed the five-o'clock news program, if she hadn't heard her father's voice. Abby stopped dead in her tracks and swung her eyes around to fix on the television set.

There was Judge Wayne Archer at a fund-raising rally with Ken Rockford at his side, surrounded by a crowd of supporters waving signs and banners. He was spouting his get-tough policy for juvenile offenders.

She'd never questioned her father's politics before. He was a conservative with high moral values. He believed right was right and wrong was wrong. When Durango had defiled his stepmother's warehouse with obscene graffiti, the judge had seen absolutely nothing wrong with teaching him a lesson by tossing him in jail for a week.

Problem was, exactly what lesson had the judge taught that young man? That you couldn't depend on your family and friends to stand by your side when you made a mistake? That authority was always right? That there was no room for either compromise or error?

No wonder Durango had felt so betrayed. Why hadn't she been able to understand this before?

As she watched the screen, someone in the crowd caught her eye and her heart froze.

It was the Monte-Carlo-driving, bad-clothes-wearing

man who had been following her. Except he now had on an expensive suit and he was whispering something in Ken's ear.

If Abby's aura had been flaming scarlet before, it now had to be vivid, angry crimson.

It was one thing to suspect her father was having her followed; it was something else entirely to have it publicly confirmed on television.

And she was going to let her father know about it in no wishy-washy, accommodating, people-pleasing terms.

Rage, vivid and clear, had her clenching her fists. Heartfelt passion for all the things she'd never known she believed in sent her storming up the stairs to her room.

Until now, she'd never felt okay about expressing her anger. She'd always viewed it as a negative force to be avoided because it upset people.

Well, enough of that. Under Durango's masterful tutelage, she had learned a lot over the past few days with the main thrust of her lessons being that it was perfectly all right to own your emotions, whether positive or negative.

It was startling for her to realize that she had a legitimate right to experience and exercise her anger. She finally grasped the true meaning of her ire and now she understood why her father encouraged her to suppress it. Anger gave her the power to say no. It took the control out of his hands and placed it firmly in hers.

The anxiety she usually felt whenever she dared cross him was gone. So was her urge to sneeze.

Abby picked up the phone and dialed her father's cell phone number the minute the rally was over.

"Hello," her father answered the phone.

No fear. In fact, she was incredibly calm. "Daddy," she said. "I know what you did and I want you to know that it won't be tolerated."

"Abby? Is that you?"

"Yes, this is your meek, obedient daughter. Except I'm no longer so meek or obedient."

"What's going on? What's happened?"

"I know you hired a guy to spy on me and I can't believe your lack of trust. Except I can. I won't have you interfere in my life anymore."

"I don't know where you got your information, but I did not send anyone to spy on you."

"Please, don't lie to me. I caught the broadcast of your rally. I saw the guy who's been following me packed in with your supporters. I'm so disappointed in you, Daddy. I won't live in your house, I've decided to move out." She didn't even know she was going to say it until she'd said it, but she'd been thinking it for a while.

All she heard on the other end was stunned silence. She took a deep breath and continued.

"In fact, I'm leaving Phoenix all together. I'm moving to Sedona."

"Moving in with Durango Creed?"

"Ha! How do you know about Durango if you haven't been spying on me?"

"Your old friend Suzanne Thompson was in Sedona on vacation and saw you at a dance club with Durango. I didn't say anything because I figured you had a right to sow your wild oats as long as the news media didn't get wind of it, but I gave you more credit than you deserved. I didn't believe you'd actually do something as stupid as letting the guy turn your head. He's behind your upsetting behavior, admit it."

"Durango has helped me see a few things, yes. Like how I'm never going to become an independent, free-thinking woman as long as I stay in Silverton Heights."

"But Abby, think this through. What about your job?"

"You got that job for me. You wanted me to have it. It was never my idea. I took it because it pleased you, because it was easier than examining my own heart and deciding what it was I wanted to do with my life."

"You've turned into Cassandra," he said bitterly. "I knew this was going to happen."

"No, Daddy, you've got it all wrong. I've finally turned into Abby."

And with that, she switched off the phone.

"I'M LEAVING PHOENIX," Abby told Durango when he came to pick her up that evening.

"What?"

"My father and I had it out."

"Was I the cause?"

"It's been a long time coming, I just didn't see it. You were right, as long as I'm living under his thumb I'll never know for sure what it is I want out of life."

"Abby…I…" Durango stared at her, his feelings a confused jumble. He'd done it. He'd accomplished his goal of unleashing her passion and getting back at her father.

He wasn't happy.

Now that he'd done it, he realized that wasn't what he wanted. What he wanted was Abby. But what would she say if she knew he'd been looking for revenge when he started up their affair?

"I don't want to bury my passion anymore. I thought I could have fun, have a sexual adventure or two and then go back to my life in Phoenix. But I realized that's impossible. I've changed, you've changed me and I'm not ashamed of my sexuality any longer."

"Oh." He didn't know how he felt about this turn of events.

"I want everything you can dish out, Durango. Don't hold back. I want you to make love to me. I want it to be the most amazing experience of my life."

"No pressure there," he laughed uneasily.

"Come on," she said, picking up her room key. "Let's go. I can't wait to get started."

"I'm starting to feel like a sex object," Durango protested jokingly. "And it's not a particularly nice feeling."

She growled and grabbed him by the collar. "You're so much more than a sex object, Durango, and you know it. You're kind and considerate. You're tender and tough. You're any woman's dream man. Now let's go. I want to come all night long."

Durango blinked. Holy cow, he'd created a monster. Shocked, he simply escorted her out to the Jeep. Was this feisty woman really his Abby? He kept peeking over at her to make sure.

"Where are we going?" she asked.

A full moon, yellow and ripe, hung heavy in the sky. A sprinkling of stars stretched out like diamonds on black velvet.

"Satan's Bridge," he said.

"I like the sound of that. Is that near a vortex?" she asked.

"It's at the epicenter of one."

"Cool."

Good God, the woman was turbocharged and bouncing around in the seat like she'd just downed a case of Red Bull. What on earth had happened to her? He wasn't so sure he could handle this dynamite side of her.

You unleashed her, buddy boy, get used to it.

He had waited until it was quite late before picking her up. He wanted to make sure they were alone on Satan's Bridge. It was almost ten o'clock by the time he parked in the National Forest parking lot, stuck the Red Rock park pass on the dashboard and pocketed his keys.

Abby helped him carry the supplies he'd brought with them. Champagne and snacks. Blankets and climbing gear and a rope sling. With the mood she was in, he was beginning to doubt the wisdom of the acrobatic moves he had planned.

The hike through the dark wasn't strenuous or dangerous and twenty minutes later, they arrived at the narrow natural stone bridge rising fifty-five feet above the ground.

The minute they set foot on the bridge, he could feel the pull of the vortex, luring them onward.

"I feel it," Abby whispered. "It's all around us."

"It's inside us, too," he said.

"I know." Her eyes were wide with wonder. "We're going to make love on this bridge."

"We're going to do more than that, Angel. I'm giving your passion the full court press."

"Bring it on," she whispered.

They laid down their supplies on the sandy ground at the entrance to the bridge. Then Durango turned, pulled Abby into his arms and kissed her in the light of the full moon.

Every time he kissed her, it got better and better. Her mouth was a furnace, stoking his desire, making him forget his nervousness. Tonight, they were going all the way.

No more teasing games.

And he planned on loving her until the sun came up and they could barely walk back to the Jeep.

This was his woman. He knew her in the marrow of his bones, in the wisdom of his blood. There was not an inch of her he would not touch, would not taste.

His hands, his lips, his tongue, his eyes would travel the lands of her body, past the boundaries of flesh and bone, into the very matrix of her soul.

She was his and he was hers. They belonged together. He would make sure she understood that.

Because his love for her was as ancient as the mesas looming around them, as wild as roving wolves, and as ferocious as the lightning that strikes across desert skies in the pitch-black storm of the loneliest night.

He undressed her in the moonlight, his fingers reverently tugging at her buttons, her zipper, her panties and shoes.

She undressed him, too, and the gasp of pleasure that escaped her lips, when she saw him fully nude at last, swelled Durango's heart with pride.

It was ego, he knew, but he loved that she appreciated his body, just as he appreciated hers.

They left their clothes in a heap on the ground. He tucked the blanket under his arm, took her hand and naked, they walked out onto the rock bridge that was little more than six feet wide. On either side of them gaped empty space, dark and mysterious.

One wrong move and they would tumble into the abyss wrapped in each other's arms.

That was why he had brought the climbing gear. Now that he'd finally found her again, he wasn't about to lose her.

The sandstone was rough and cool beneath their bare feet. He spread out the blanket, had her sit down, then went back for the ropes and the pulleys and chains. He'd already been here earlier in the day and rigged up the hardware into the rocks. He'd tested it numerous times to make sure it was completely secure. What they were about to do was less dangerous than hang gliding but ten times more thrilling.

Or at least he hoped so. He had never done this before.

Abby watched him connect the equipment. "We're going to make love up here."

"Yes."

"We could die," she said.

"Do you trust me?" he asked.

She met his eyes, moistened her lips until they glistened wetly in the moon glow. She knew tonight would be the pinnacle of their time together. There was no hesitation in her voice when she murmured, "Yes."

He attached cables to the bolts centered in the rocks on both sides of the bridge. He added pulleys and the rope swing. Then he attached a climbing harness around his waist and secured it to the riggings and brought the second harness over to Abby.

"Stand up."

She did and he strapped the nylon contraption around her beautiful bare waist.

When he had completed his task, she reached forward to gently cup his groin. His cock rose to greet her tender touch. He had broken through her civilized shell and released the primal woman within.

He was overwhelmed.

Their mouths met and his hands flew to her exposed skin. She was hot. Hot with passion and energy and feminine power. Durango looked at his fingers then, making sure they weren't seared to the bone.

Slowly Abby sank to the blanket, taking his arm, taking him with her. Their kissing continued but grew more demanding.

Abby was beyond beauty to him. She was pure intellect and pure animal. Her cool reserve had completely melted, her inner instincts bucking against all the stuffy edicts of her society. She caressed his body without caution or fear, all her doubts, all her hesitation gone.

She filled his past as much as she filled his present

and, he hoped, his future. He had never before been so physically possessed by a woman. Her tongue was an exquisite instrument of torture, her fingers a delicate tool of delicious anguish.

The boldness.

The audacity.

The daring.

She had given up her facade, given in to her real self, surrendered to the connection of passion flowing out of the air, mixing and vibrating with her blood.

They were situated directly above a dominant electromagnetic vortex. The yin and the yang of force fields. Masculine and feminine combined for the ultimate in balance and power and strength. Neither was whole without the other.

She straddled him, legs locked around his waist, her sweet sex pressed against his pelvic bone. His cock pulsated, aching to be inside. Abby rocked and her movements shook the bridge beneath them.

The smooth stone vibrated.

He was exalted. Her body was a goddesslike temple, something to revere and worship.

Their desire escalated as the energy swirled and coalesced within and around them. They nibbled and suckled and licked each other, tasting the salt of their skin, listening to the huskiness of their ragged breathing, inhaling each other's earthy scents.

Durango felt as if he'd opened the sacred door to a treasured vault and the treasures were immense, but so was the price. Over the years he had carefully built his defenses.

He'd told himself he didn't need to belong to a place as hidebound and narrow-minded as Silverton Heights. He'd convinced himself he was a lone wolf who needed no one. He'd conned his own ego into believing he didn't care what people thought of him.

Stubbornly he'd clung to the landmarks of the independent trail he'd blazed. But what had helped him in the early stages of his life, had hurt him later on. He'd kept others at a distance, raising his guard.

Paradoxically, he'd found safety in risk taking, found a sort of acceptance in defying the norm.

But deep down inside, his equilibrium had been off. Something had always been amiss.

Until now.

Their lips navigated skin terrain with measured, meticulous gestures, stopping now and again to finger the definition of an erogenous zone, to pry and discover more and more layers of sensation.

They whispered ramblingly to each other, lips muted against breasts, necks, belly grottos.

She moaned slowly.

He groaned loudly.

The rock surface beneath the thin woolen blanket was hard but they did not notice.

He kissed her nipples, massaged her breasts. She stroked his shaft, fondled his testicles. He licked a trail from her nipples down her taunt abdomen to her inner thighs. She quivered and grabbed his hands with both of hers.

"Take me, Durango, take me now," she begged.

But he refused. "It's too soon," he whispered, and gently kissed her mouth.

He wanted their joining to be the ultimate experience. For her, for him, for them both. But it pleased him to know he had roused her to such an agitated state that she was writhing and bucking against his lips. What could delight a man more than moving the woman he loves?

If only he could bring her up here every night, to this level of rapture. Clasp her by the soul and escort her to that elongated instant of spontaneous ecstasy.

She leaned over him, her breasts brushing provocatively against his chest, and kissed him. He inhaled her breath, warm as his own.

Then she slipped down the length of his body and, before he had the presence of mind to stop her, she wrapped her hot, willing mouth around him.

"No," he insisted, and tenderly raised her chin, forcing her to look at him. "If you do that I won't last five seconds."

"I don't care."

"I do. I want us both to come together."

"What next?" she asked, breathlessly panting as their gazes feasted on each other.

He gave her his best, wicked, lopsided grin. "It's time," he said, "for the swing."

11

THEY WERE IN A SEX SWING.

Suspended fifty-five feet above the earth. The swing was attached to strong cables anchored into the rock with heavy bolts and a series of pulleys. They were also wearing climbing harnesses that were attached to both the bridge and either side of the stone canyon walls.

Durango was an expert climber. For years he had been engaging in extreme sports. He knew exactly what he was doing. There was no way they would get hurt.

Abby knew this was going to be the most erotically charged experience of her life.

Durango was lying back in the rope swing in a semireclining position, Abby straddling him. The individual nylon climbing harnesses snugged around both of their waists.

Every time she moved, the swing rocked.

It was an indescribable sensation.

Pushing with her knees against the rope, she sent the swing moving faster. She felt daring and dangerous, passionate and vibrant. At long last, she truly knew who she was.

She was a woman who seized life by the throat and squeezed every ounce of opportunity from it. She'd spent too many years hiding from herself. She had a lot of catching up to do.

"Easy, Angel," Durango said. "For a woman who used to hate rocking the boat, you've taken quite a fancy to rocking this swing."

"It feels like utopia. Nothing below us, nothing pressing on us. Just you and me and nature and the vortex. Swinging and swirling and swaying."

"Don't forget the rope and the harnesses and the cables. While I've made certain the riggings are secure, we *are* engaging in an extreme sport."

"Think it will ever become an event in the Olympics?" she teased. "We could take the gold."

She began moving over the top of him, sliding back and forward over his lean, muscular frame, making the minute space between them rocket-hot with her ceaseless action. Durango's head was thrown back, exposing his throat. His glossy black hair spilled down his neck.

The slippery friction rolled and slid, sucking and pressing every dip and swell of their sultry skin. Soon, her skin merged with his so that it became impossible to define where one gliding and rolling body began and the other ended.

The swing swayed rhythmically.

It felt gloriously out of control.

Durango raised his head and took one of her full breasts into his mouth. She moaned softly as his tongue did wicked things to her nipple.

She reached down to capture his shaft between her thumb and index finger. She applied a firm but gentle pressure, then used the pulsating head to caress the outside of her womanhood. She moved her body intuitively, exploring all kinds of touches.

When she was slick and hot, Abby inserted the tip of him inside her and squeezed him tight within her. He made a sound of startled pleasure.

"Where did you learn that?"

She laughed. "I just made it up."

"Well, keep the imagination coming."

"And coming and coming and coming."

"You're irredeemable."

"And you like me that way." She -tickled him lightly across the ribs.

"Angel, I like you any way I can get you."

She leaned over then and kissed him, the tip of him still inside her. She felt totally relaxed, which was quite odd considering the position they were in.

But she trusted Durango and knew that she was safe here with him.

The night's breeze cooled their heated skin. The full moon bathed them in a splash of grand desert light. The chains creaked, echoing softly through the darkened canyon below.

Gradually she lowered herself down until she was completely impaled on Durango's rigid shaft. She hissed out her breath, amazed at the way he filled her up.

She moved fluidly, up and down his erection. She stared into his face, got lost in his heart-stopping ebony eyes.

He rocked his hips in time to her movements. The swing went crazy, gyrating in the midnight air.

Using long, sinuous, thrusting motions, Abby let him go all the way out and then all the way back in. Reaching up, she grabbed hold of the chains above her to help her thrust harder. The chains were cold and dry against her slick, heated palms.

Even though she was doing all the work, she could sense Durango's arousal rising along with her own.

She constricted her inner muscles around him again, tightening and contracting around his pounding erection. Milking him hard with her softness.

"Yes," he screamed, and the sound erupted into the night. "Yes, Angel, yes."

His hands shot out and he grasped her hips, pulling her down harder. The swing twisted and bucked. He braced his feet against the ropes and matched her thrusts.

"Faster," she cried.

They were spinning, turning, lost in a whirl of magic and power, caught up in their boldness and daring. The world belonged to them. They owned it.

And when they came, they came together, crying each other's name over and over into the darkness.

OKAY, SHE WAS GOING to take Durango's advice and dial down her enthusiasm a notch. She was not going to pressure Jackson for sex.

So when Jackson called and asked her to meet him on Cathedral Rock at midnight, she acted nonchalant and wouldn't make any promises that she would be there, even though her heart was thumping so loudly she feared he might actually hear it through the phone lines.

She didn't dress in her usual seductive clothing. In fact, she borrowed from Abby, rummaging around in her dresser drawers until she found the perfect outfit. Tailored slacks, button-down blue silk blouse, sensible walking shoes.

Tess arrived at Cathedral Rock ten minutes after midnight. The hike wasn't too spooky, with the full moon as her guide. She was testing him. Would Jackson still be there? Or had he already given up on her because she was late? The answer would tell her a lot about his seriousness.

Before she reached the top of the mesa, she could hear the soft strains of music and she smiled to herself. He must have talked to Abby. How else could he have known she was a huge Celine Dion fan?

Apparently, he was deadly serious about his devotion to pleasing her. Give the man an A for effort.

When she arrived at the top of the trailhead, her heart started to race. There, in the middle of the mesa, Jackson had set up a card table with a white linen tablecloth, flickering candles and an assortment of aphrodisiacs from truffles to caviar to chocolate.

Holy moly, he was pulling out the big guns. It had taken quite an effort, hauling everything up here.

Tess was touched by his grand gesture. It made a girl feel special.

Jackson was decked out in a tuxedo. He stepped toward her, hand outstretched.

Shyly Tess hung back, partly in homage to Durango's cautious advice but also because she was suddenly overcome with a quiet stillness that she never knew lived inside her.

Her brazenness vanished under the tender expression in Jackson's eyes. Gone was her self-assured boldness, her impudent self. Where was the saucy wench who wanted sex and lots of it?

Replaced. By a woman who was secretly hoping for something more.

''Tess,'' he murmured, and pulled out a chair for her to sit.

He popped the cork on a bottle of champagne. They sat dining as if they were at a five-star restaurant in Paris instead of a mesa top in Sedona.

The air swirled around them, thick and aromatic with the scent of piñon pine. They drank a toast to the vortex, then set down their glasses. Tess eyed the exotic nibbles of food spread out before them.

"Caviar?" He spooned up a lob of caviar on a sesame-seed cracker and fed it to her with his fingers.

"What are you hungry for?" she asked after she'd eaten the delicious delicacy and licked her lips.

"For this." Jackson leaned across the table, took her chin in his palm and raised her face to meet his. Slowly, teasingly, his lips descended upon hers.

She pulled back.

"I don't think we should be doing this," she said. "It's not a good idea."

"That wasn't what you were saying last night."

"Last night I had too much schnapps. My judgment was clouded."

"So have some more champagne." He flicked his tongue along her jaw and it was all she could do not to throw her arms around him and take him right there.

"I need to keep my wits about me."

"Why's that?"

"Because you make me nervous."

"And why is that."

"Dammit, what is this? Twenty questions."

"Nope, twenty kisses."

His mouth found hers again. There was something comforting in the way he kissed. Rather old-fashioned and courtly. He held her close as if she was the most precious thing he'd ever touched.

She felt the shimmering heat in her fingers and toes, experienced the fevered hot wetness in her mouth. Her stomach, the very core of her womanhood, came alive beneath his touch.

Never had any kiss tasted so sweet, so intense, so vital.

Ten glasses of the finest champagne could not have equaled the intoxicating power of his lips. A hundred romantic ballads could not have produced music as mesmerizing as Jackson's steady breathing. Ten thousand lit candles could not have compared with the sultry blaze in his brown eyes.

All of this for her.

And she felt positively demure, basking in his attention.

While his tongue entwined with hers, his hands were busy easing open the buttons of her shirt.

Ah, to hell with the thrill of the chase, she thought. She was going to let him have his way, because she wanted him as much as he wanted her.

Tess did not protest when his fingers pushed beneath her bra and gently caressed her pink nipple buds. Closing her eyes, she rode the wave, acutely aware of every minute sensation.

The feel of his callused palm against her skin, the succulent taste of his mouth, the scent of his freshly shampooed hair triggered an immediate response.

More. More. She wanted more.

Durango had advised her to hold back, but she could not. Jackson was everything she wanted.

Moaning softly, Tess tilted her head, exposing her bare neck to him.

He nibbled her throbbing pulse points. The sensation sent aching spikes of awareness flooding her whole body. She moaned again, overcome with the deliciousness of it all.

Maybe things really could work out between them.

Tess took the tentative faith and tucked it away inside her. Then his mouth was at her breast and she forgot everything but the moment.

Their kissing reached a fevered pitch and they were taken over by a force as old as time. The maelstrom of the vortex stoked their mounting passion.

Jackson swept the food from the table. The dishes clattered in a heap to the stone below. Neither of them cared. She sucked in her breath at the sudden shock of his passion.

He whisked off her clothes. She helped him shuck the tuxedo.

It was wonderful, all of it. The probing and the touching. The smell of man and champagne.

''What's your pleasure,'' he whispered as if he held the key to a treasure chest of phenomenal things and all she had to do was ask and her heart's desire would magically appear.

She didn't speak, but guided his penis where she

wanted it to go. Meanwhile, his lips were everywhere, at her cheek, her nose, her eyelids.

She hesitated. Was this right? It couldn't be otherwise, it felt so good.

"I want you," he said, sensing her mental doubts and kissing her chin.

Her optimism soared. Her protective shell cracked, just the teeniest bit.

Maybe, maybe.

After all, she'd never felt this way before. She had heard it sung about in love songs, read about it in romance novels, but this heartfelt power had never been a part of her reality.

It didn't have to include tomorrow. She had no expectations beyond tonight. But for now this feeling was so true and real she could not deny it.

They were making love on top of the mesa in the moonlight, stripped bare of all pretenses.

It aroused Tess to unthinkable heights. Decadent. Sinful. Wickedly indulgent.

Jackson found a grape squashed underneath his bottom and swept it away.

Tess giggled.

"You think that's funny?"

"Uh-huh." She nodded.

"I'll show you funny," Jackson said, and lightly tickled her.

"Oh, no, stop!" She squirmed.

"How about here?" He trailed a hand along her hip walking his fingers down her thigh.

"Wow."

"Does this tickle?"

"Hmm, no, that doesn't tickle."

"What does it feel like?"

"Good. Really really good."

"And this."

"Ohh."

"How about this?"

"Stop talking." She reached up, threaded her fingers through his hair and pulled his face down to her mouth.

Their lovemaking was wild, frantic, filled with the peril of getting caught, the urgency of rushing. It was basic and hungry and primitive.

He placed her astride his body and Tess rode him, thrilling in her savage sexuality.

She peered down into his face, into those deep and murky eyes and saw herself reflected there.

Saw love.

It scared Tess and healed her all at the same time.

"Jackson," she cried, loud and throaty as she crested on the throes of her orgasm. "Jackson, Jackson, Jackson."

"Yes, luv, yes."

His hands clamped around her hips, held her pinned in place upon his male hardness. Waves of ecstasy slammed into her, tripping through her body with a mind-shattering force.

The incredible power unbalanced her, sent her spinning into oblivion. His guttural cries told her that Jackson had joined her in completion.

Ah, Tess thought. It was true what they said. There was no sex like vortex sex.

ON THE FOLLOWING DAY, Abby signed up for Sunrise Tours first Freefall adventure with Durango as her guide. Last night, she'd had an erotic sexual experience she'd never forget. Now she was ready to tackle the ultimate physical high—skydiving.

Every muscle in her body was already sore and aching, but in a good way. She marveled at the changes in her, both in her body and her mind. Thanks to Durango and her own willingness to push her boundaries, she was finally coming into her own.

She had stood up to her father. She had made a decision to move to Sedona to explore a possible future with Durango. *She* had made love in a sex swing suspended from a fifty-five-foot rock bridge in the middle of the night.

It didn't get much more passionate than that.

They sat in the cargo hold of the plane, wearing jumpsuits and strapped into their tandem harnesses, the two of them one once more. Durango winked and reached over to lightly squeeze her hand.

This was big. The final test of her determination to be who she truly was.

Already she was growing to love the sky as much as Durango did. It beckoned to her, whispered her name. Her heart thudded. She felt wonderful, but trembled inside.

"How many times have you skydived?" she asked.

"Relax, Angel. I'm a certified instructor."

"You're so good at any and everything out there," she said.

"Keeps the demons at bay."

"Is that why you do it?"

"You're doing one hell of a job keeping up with me." He grinned and ignored her question. Why was he such a thrill seeker. What pain did it salve? "I can't stop thinking about last night. You were incredible."

"Thank you." She accepted his compliment and didn't once feel the urge to sneeze.

"We're over the drop zone," the pilot called over his shoulder to them.

"This is it."

As one, they got to their feet and edged toward the door. Durango opened the hatch. Invigoratingly cold air blasted into the cabin. Abby peered out, saw puffy white clouds rolling by, inviting them to jump.

"Are you ready to freefall, Angel? Are you sure you're ready for this?"

"Ready!" she sang out, her blood rushing, swelling, pounding headlong through her veins.

The pilot cut the engine. The silence was almost deafening as they glided along. Only the sound of their breathing filled the small plane.

Together, they climbed out onto the strut and held on tight in the eighty-mile-per-hour wind. Her pulse was racing as fast as it had the night before when she and Durango had made crazy, vortex love.

Memories of that experience danced in her head, mingled with the adrenaline spiking through her stomach. She thought of how Durango had shown her just how much she meant to him.

"Let go," he whispered into her ear.

Abby squeezed her eyes closed. She trusted him the way she'd been unable to trust him ten years ago.

She turned loose.

And they were freefalling.

Tumbling, tripping, hurtling toward the ground at an incredible speed. The rush was intensely wonderful. The earth sucked them down.

She forced her eyes open and smiled into Durango's face. They were moving so fast his cheeks were vibrating in the wind. She figured hers were too.

Down, down, down they fell.

Lingering fears swelled. She wasn't alone, she reminded herself. Durango was harnessed to her. In tandem. Two as one, two as one, two as one.

The jump went by blindingly fast.

At four thousand feet above the ground, Durango pulled the rip cord. The bright orange parachute shot out behind them, billowing into a brilliant canopy of vibrant triumphant.

Their descent slowed, everything changed.

Gone was the mad rush of sensation and in its place was utter tranquility.

They floated, suspended, drifting on air. Other than the flapping of the parachute in the wind, there was only silence.

A deep, thoughtful silence that they shared.

Down, down, down they drifted, while Abby's spirit soared at the possibilities of the future. She could be anything she wanted to be. Go anywhere she wanted to go. She was no longer defined by the demands and expectations of other people.

She'd done it. She'd proved herself, found her inner passion. She was no longer go-with-the-flow Abby, hiding her true self from herself. She'd learned to mix her agreeable disposition with a newfound talent for emotional strength and endurance.

She no longer feared loss or separation from her home and her community. She had discovered that maybe she could make a difference in her own life, that it paid to get energized, involved. She was more powerful than she had ever dreamed.

Freefalling into a whole wide world far beyond her father's circle of influence. A world not controlled by emotion like Cassandra's, but instead, defined by it.

They dropped together with precision accuracy and landed softly on the ground. It would have been a perfect touchdown except for one very distracting detail.

The moment their feet hit the earth, they were mobbed by media people spilling out of news vans, dragging camera crews behind them, all demanding details about the front-page picture in the sleaziest tabloid magazine ever to see ink.

The Confidential Inquisitor.

A picture that depicted gubernatorial candidate Judge Archer's daughter having sex in a rope swing dangling from Satan's Bridge with the sexiest bad-boy black-sheep rake this side of Phoenix.

12

"NO COMMENT," Durango repeatedly told reporters as he grimly hustled Abby to his Jeep.

The euphoria he'd experienced over their perfect tandem jump disintegrated in the face of reality. The explicit details of their envelope-pushing affair had morphed into a gossip-rag pictorial.

He cringed.

Judge Archer might end up shamed over his daughter's sizzling scandal, but it was Abby who was really going to suffer the consequences.

And it was all his fault. Durango felt lower than snail slime.

He had to get Abby out of here, had to protect her from the prying eyes of curiosity seekers. He slammed the Jeep in gear, almost crunching the toes of one particularly aggressive newsman who wouldn't get out of his way.

Abby was pale and visibly shaken. Someone had shoved the front page of the paper into her hand. She was still holding it, staring numbly down at the damning photograph.

"Give me that." Durango jerked the vile gossip rag from her hand and pitched it into the back seat.

"Who…who…" She shook her head and swallowed back the tears he heard stuck in her throat. "Who took these pictures?"

"The paparazzi guy?"

"But he wasn't a paparazzi guy," Abby said. "He was working for my father. Daddy might have me followed so he could find out what I was up to, but he would make damned sure none of it ever got into the papers."

"I'm sorry," he said, his gut tearing him into two pieces.

"It's not your fault."

"Yes it is. If I hadn't insisted on pushing you into way-out sex, none of this would have happened."

Guilt weighed heavily on his conscience. Once he had started this seduction, he'd realized how much he still loved her and his goal had become all about helping Abby find herself.

But in the beginning, his motives had been less than honorable. He *had* wanted revenge against her father, but he didn't want her misinterpreting the chain of events. He had to find a way to explain himself. Unfortunately, this stupid gossip scandal muddied the waters.

"Hey," she protested. "No finger-pointing. This was as much my idea as yours." She groaned and dropped her head into her hands. "Daddy is going to be livid."

The Jeep's radio was tuned on low to the news talk station. Neither of them was paying the broadcast any attention until the announcer said, "This hour we're dissecting today's amusing, embarrassing political sex scandal involving gubernatorial candidate Judge Wayne Archer's daughter."

"Dammit," Durango said, and made a move to snap off the radio.

"No wait," Abby said and raised a hand. "I need to hear how bad this is."

"Are you sure?"

She clenched her jaw and nodded.

"Joining us today is feature writer and political columnist from *Arizona* magazine, Eric Provost. Welcome, Eric, and thanks for joining us."

"Thanks for having me, Dave," Eric replied.

Abby frowned. "Eric Provost? Isn't he the guy who did the story on your Outward Bound program?"

Durango nodded. "Listen Abby, there's something I've got to tell you."

"Shh." She waved a hand, her ears straining to hear what Eric had to say.

Reluctantly Durango turned up the volume.

"So Eric, what do you think of this morning's front page of the *Confidential Inquisitor?*"

"Dave, I think it's hysterical. Here's Judge You're-responsible-for-the-actions-of-your-children Archer, who's running on a get-tough platform on juvenile crime, eating crow because his daughter has been caught on camera doing some pretty lewd and lascivious acts in public, not to mention defiling one of Sedona's natural treasures.''

"Great going, Eric," Durango muttered. "Now the environmentalists will be up in arms, too."

Abby had her fingers knotted in her lap and he bet she was trying hard not to cry.

His masculine urge to protect her at all costs swept over him. He reached for the off button. "This is upsetting you. It's outta here."

"No," she snapped. "I have to know what Daddy is up against. I have to know exactly how bad this is going to get."

Durango blew out a breath. He wanted to offer her comfort, but she didn't seem to be in the mood to let him. Besides, he was tainted. He still hadn't unburdened his guilt to her, and now he didn't know how he was ever going to do it. Anything he said at this point would end up looking like too little, too late.

It was too little, too late.

"Do you know what I find most fittingly ironic about this whole situation?" Eric Provost asked the talk-show host.

"What's that, Eric?"

"The guy in the photograph with Abby Archer is a man by the name of Durango Creed. Ten years ago Judge Archer jailed him on a minor teenage infraction and Durango's relationship with his entire family was irretrievably broken over the incident.''

"Interesting sidebar," Dave, the talk-show host, commented.

Slowly Abby turned her head toward Durango.

"Hey, Durango, buddy, if you're listening out there, way to get revenge for the week of your life Judge Archer wasted in that Phoenix county jail." Eric's voice oozed from the radio as deadly as toxic sludge. "Soiling the judge's daughter was a stroke of brilliance. Hit him right where it hurts, in his own backyard. Show the guy up for the hypocrite he is."

"Ouch!" The announcer chuckled. "You know that's gotta hurt."

"Play with fire, Dave, and you're gonna get burned."

"How do you think this will affect the judge's bid for office?" Dave asked.

"You can bet your ballot his opponent Mack Woodruff, just got a bump up in his approval rating and hey, as far as I'm concerned, so did Durango Creed. Only time will tell the larger impact on the judge's career."

"Durango?" Abby's voice was reedy, accusatory. "Is this why you wanted to turn off the radio? You were afraid your friend was going to spill your secret, like he just did."

He couldn't look at her. Couldn't bear to see the

hurt in her eyes and know he'd been the one to put it there. "Abby, I…" he started, but couldn't finish.

"Did you just have sex with me to get revenge against my father." The anguish in her voice was killing him.

"It's not like that."

"What *is* it like?"

He bit down on the inside of his cheek.

"Look at me, Durango."

He wasn't a coward. He had no choice but to face up to what he'd done and pray she could find it in her heart to forgive him. He met her eyes. Hurt and disbelief shimmered as unshed tears in those wide hazel eyes.

"It's true, isn't it. You did sleep with me to get revenge against my father!"

"In the beginning it might have started out that way," he admitted. "But watching you open up to your passion, seeing you come into your own, completely changed my motives. You've got to believe me, Abby. I never meant to cause you this kind of grief."

"Oh save it. I don't want to hear anymore."

"Abby," he said quietly, "I deserve every bit of your anger, but this you've got to know deep in your heart. I care about you."

"This is a real crappy way of showing it, Durango, ruining my dad's career. Stop the Jeep. I want to get out."

"Angel, be reasonable. I can't leave you here in the middle of nowhere."

"I'm through being reasonable, in case you haven't noticed. You're the one who showed me how. And don't worry about abandoning me at the roadside— the media frenzy trailing after us should be along soon, I'm sure they will be more than happy to give me a ride for my side of the story. Oh, and for the record, I don't ever want to see you again."

HEART LURCHING into her breastbone, legs quivering, Abby leaped out of the Jeep the minute Durango pulled over.

"Abby," Durango pleaded. "Please, you've got to hear me out."

Her hands shook with fury as she grabbed the gossip magazine from the back seat and shook it under his nose. "Exactly how much did you get paid to publicly humiliate me?"

She'd known all along he harbored a grudge against her dad, against the good people of Silverton Heights. He'd made no bones about that fact. Really, she shouldn't be surprised or hurt, but sadly she was.

Never, in a million aeons, would she have suspected he could be so coldly calculating as to hire some low-life scum to follow them and photograph them in the throes of an intimate moment.

And to think she'd been spinning *what if* fantasies

about their future. That she'd planned on moving to Sedona for him.

What a fool she'd been.

Durango got out of the Jeep, slammed the door hard behind him. He snatched the gossip rag from her hands and furiously started shredding it to pieces.

"I—" *shred* "—did—" *shred* "—not—" *shred* "—hire anyone to follow and photograph us." He balled up the tattered pieces and flung the confetti into the Jeep.

The sun beat down. The utter silence swirling from the red rock mesas surrounding them was deafening.

"And if you believe that about me," he continued, "there's no hope for us at all."

Abby glared at him, hard and long.

Durango flinched but did not shrink back under the force of her ire.

"You really don't want to hear what I have to say right now," she said. "I advise you to get into your Jeep and drive away before I say something I'll regret to my dying day."

"Go ahead." He hardened his jaw. "Let me have it. I deserve the best you can dish out."

Instead, Abby turned on her heel and started walking away from him.

"Running away isn't the answer," Durango called after her. "Stay and fight this out with me. I know you've learned it's better to embrace conflict than hide from it."

She did not reply, could not reply because if she did she feared she would burst into tears, and she wasn't about to give him the satisfaction of seeing her cry.

"Abby, please." He jogged to catch up.

She looked down, instead of over at him, and noticed her shoes were kicking up soft billows of red sand as she walked.

He gently took her by the elbow, forced her to stop walking and spun her around to face him. "You've got to let me make this up to you."

She jerked her elbow away, the same elbow that still sported the bandage he'd so tenderly applied only a couple of days before, and sank her hands on her hips.

"Some things can't be forgiven, Durango. Surely you know that," she said darkly.

"What do you mean?" His eyes darted over her face.

She'd never seen him nervous, but he looked damned scared.

"You've never been able to fully forgive me or my dad or even your own father for what happened when you were eighteen. You were wronged, yes. You were still grieving your mother, we all understand that. But you've got to let go of the past. You've been hiding out in Sedona, telling yourself you're self-reliant and free, that you don't need to follow the rules or fit in with society's norms. You tempt fate. You pride yourself on boldly going where few men have gone before. But the truth is, you're prideful, uncompromising and stubborn. But most of all, you're chicken.''

''Chicken?''

''Face it, you're a fraud. You're as scared of being accepted by everyone else as I was afraid of exploring my passionate side.''

''Abby.'' He reached out a hand to her. His voice cracked.

While the sight of her big tough Durango on the verge of losing his composure wrenched at her, Abby stubbornly hardened her resolve against him.

''How can I fix this?'' he asked, anguish twisting his handsome features. He looked sadder and wiser. Abby toughened her heart. She wasn't going to forgive that easily.

''You've not only hurt me, but my father's reputation might be ruined. I don't think you can make up for that.''

Anger flared in his eyes, edging out his guilt and shame. ''Okay fine. If you can't or won't forgive me, that's your prerogative. But no matter how you feel about me, one thing remains true and there's nothing you can do to change it.''

''And what's that?'' she snapped.

''I'm in love with you,'' he said.

Then he turned, stalked back to the Jeep and drove away, leaving Abby standing there more confused and miserable than ever.

TRUE. Every single thing Abby had said about him was true.

He was prideful and uncompromising and stubborn. And he was too chicken to ask for forgiveness from the people he'd been convinced had wronged him and he'd been too chicken to bestow forgiveness on them in return.

He had to make amends. Whatever it took to repair Abby and the judge's situation, he would do it. He was going to discover who took that picture.

Calling in an old favor, he got a pilot friend of his to fly him directly to Clearfork, California, the home offices of the *Confidential Inquisitor*. He wanted answers and he wanted them now and he wasn't going to quit until he got them.

Once in California, Durango had to threaten the tabloid with a lawsuit, but eventually they told him that the photographer was a man by the name of Lance Peabody who made a living off catching politicians and their families with their pants down. Peabody, conveniently enough, lived in Phoenix.

When Durango rang Lance Peabody's doorbell the next morning, he wasn't surprised when the man who answered the door turned out to be the Van Halen T-shirt guy.

The minute he recognized him, Peabody tried to slam the door closed, but Durango was already shouldering his way inside. Taking on his best bad-boy countenance, he loomed threateningly over the much smaller guy.

"Who hired you to take those pictures of Judge Archer's daughter?" He moved menacingly toward Peabody.

The middle-aged photographer backed up until he ran into his living-room wall. He raised his palms defensively. "Hey, pal, if you two hadn't been doing the humpty in a public place there wouldn't have been anything to photograph. You set yourselves up. Slam dunk for me, scandal for the hot chick."

It took all of Durango's self-control not to cold-cock the little rat. "Who put you up to it?"

"I never reveal my sources. It would be professional suicide."

"I'll double whatever you were paid," Durango said, reaching into his pocket for a wad of cash.

That promise sold out Peabody's loyalty without a quibble. "Guy by the name of Ken Rockford hired me," he said, once Durango had counted out enough twenties to make two grand.

It was easily worth it, to earn a second chance with Abby.

"Ken Rockford? Are you sure?" Durango frowned. "But he's Judge Archer's campaign manager. Why would Judge Archer want to cause a scandal concerning his own daughter?"

Peabody smiled. "Now that's the real interestin' part. Ken Rockford is secretly working for Mack Woodruff to sabotage the Archer campaign."

"What's Rockford gaining from all this?" Durango asked.

"It's got something to do with the state highway zoning laws," Peabody explained. "Woodruff wants to change the law so he can build a new highway. Rockford's family owns land near where the proposed highway will be built. It'll triple his property value. Archer opposes the new highway."

"Ah," Durango said. Now that he had answers, it was time to pay a visit to the illustrious Judge Archer.

13

SHE WAS NOT GOING to cry. Abby refused to let him hurt her that much.

The bastard.

Is that fair, Abby? niggled her conscience. *To crucify Durango for his motives when you wanted nothing more than to have a fling with him so you could stop fantasizing about him? He used you, yes. But face it, you used him too. You are not guiltless.*

Moaning softly, she curled in a fetal position on her bed at the Tranquility Spa, uncertain what to do next. She had no idea where Tess had gone to. Her father had been calling repeatedly and leaving urgent voice-mail messages asking her to call him back, but she wasn't up to facing him.

Not yet.

How could she tell the man who had always been her Rock of Gibraltar that she had made a horrible, horrible mistake and he was going to be the one to suffer the consequences?

How could she have been so foolish? So gullible? This wasn't like her. But she had been vulnerable after getting ditched by Ken and then she had made the mistake of listening to Cassandra and Tess.

But she couldn't blame them either. There had been a spark of rebellion simmering inside her for years, just waiting for the opportunity to burst into flames.

And burst she had. Like a moth to a lantern, wings singed.

She thought of that unholy photograph on the front of the tabloid, closed her eyes and groaned aloud. She thought of the smug radio interviewer. The talk-show host and the guest had enjoyed making fun of her. To them, her life was nothing but a big fat joke.

Her greatest fear had officially come to pass. She'd stupidly followed her passion and it had led her into temptation, and that temptation had brought about what she feared most in life.

Being disconnected from those she loved.

The only thing she'd ever really wanted, peace of mind and wholeness, seemed lost to her forever.

Here was her quandary. Accept that her life had changed irrevocably and she was the cause. Or put this awful passion back in the box, go home to her father, try her best to earn his forgiveness and forget she'd ever met Durango Creed.

It should have been an easy decision. Equanimity versus chaos. She was surprised to discover that it was not.

The door opened and Tess sauntered in.

"Tess?" Hugging her pillow to her chest, Abby sat

up and blinked at her friend who drifted into their room with a beatific smile on her face.

"Hmm?"

"Are you all right?"

"Uh-huh," Tess said dreamily and sat down on the edge of her bed.

"You look…"

"Yes?"

"Well, calm and tranquil."

"I feel calm and tranquil."

"This is too spooky and totally unlike you." Abby furrowed her brow.

"I feel unlike me." Tess beamed.

"What's happened? Are you all right?" Abby felt alarmed. With her world knocked out of control the one thing she had been counting on was for Tess to remain her same sassy self. Tess had always been able to cheer her up when no one else could.

"Never been better." Tess softly hummed a romantic love song.

"Were you with Jackson?"

"Uh-huh."

"Wait a minute." Abby grinned and snapped her fingers. Now she had the answer to her friend's mysterious transformation. "Did you get laid last night?"

"No," Tess whispered reverently. "I got made love to. Last night, this morning and lots of times in between."

"Made love?" Abby had never heard Tess use those words to describe sex.

"It was incredible. No man has ever looked at me that way. Like I'm something really special."

"But you are special!"

"No one else but you has ever made me feel special. Not even my parents."

"That's wonderful that Jackson makes you feel so good."

Tess stopped humming. The expression on her face went from dreamy to unsettled. "Is it really?"

"Of course it is."

"Even if I'm changing?"

"All change isn't bad. Maybe you're just growing into your womanhood."

Tess bit down on her bottom lip. "I'm afraid it might be more than that. Abby, I want to be with him so badly."

"Then be with him."

"I've never felt this way before and I'm scared."

"What are you scared of?"

"You know my family." Tess waved a hand. "We're such a mess."

"Everyone's family is a mess. This is about you, not them. Why are you afraid?"

"I'm nervous about the way he's changing me. I act differently when I'm around him. I feel differently."

Abby certainly understood that fear. Durango had

changed her in inexplicable ways and now there was no way to get the old Abby back. Where in the hell was she supposed to go from here?

"He makes me feel so warm and tender inside I'm afraid of losing my toughness, you know," Tess said softly, "I'm afraid of losing the thing that makes me, me."

Abby was just the opposite. Durango made her feel so strong and brave she was afraid of losing her softness. But Durango was out of her life for good now, she had nothing more to worry about on that score.

Except for the lonely aching deep within her heart.

"I think I could really get serious about Jackson. There. I said it."

"You? Miss Commitment-phobe? Get serious about a guy?"

Tess shrugged. "Crazy, I know."

"Have you told Jackson this?"

Tess looked aghast. "And risk getting my heart stomped to smithereens? Nothing doing."

"Then how do you expect to get serious about him?" Abby asked, exasperated. One of them should at least get the man they wanted.

"It's a stupid dream. He's a stuntman from Australia."

"So?"

"I don't even have a passport."

"Come on, Tess, what's the real reason you're holding back?"

"Okay." Tess blew out her breath. "I'm worried I won't be enough for him. He's got groupies and he travels with his job and those long-distance things don't work, as evidenced by how boarding school alienated me from my family."

"Maybe he'll quit the movie business for you."

"You think?" Tess perked up.

"And even if he doesn't quit, maybe you can just learn to trust him."

Like you trusted Durango?

Bad example. Before she had a chance to retract her statement, Tess was headed for the door. "Thanks, Ab, you've been a great help. I'm off to lay my heart on the line. Hang around in case it doesn't go well, okay?"

"Don't worry, Tess. Men may come and men may go, but I'll be here for you always."

THE NEXT MORNING Durango marched into Judge Archer's office and laid out the paper trail of Ken Rockford's duplicity that Lance Peabody had provided him.

Judge Wayne Archer stared with stony-faced accusation until he reviewed the evidence. "Where did you get this?"

"Lance Peabody. The guy Ken hired to spy on Abby for Mack Woodruff, to ruin her reputation."

Judge Archer peered down the end of his reading

glasses. "From the external looks of things, I'd say *you* were the guy who ruined my daughter."

Durango squarely met the older man's steely eyes. "I'm sorry if I caused you any embarrassment, sir. It was never my intention to hurt your daughter."

"But I know you wanted to get back at me. For sticking you in jail when you were a kid."

"There was an element of that, yes. But I love Abby and I would do anything for her. Including tracking down the man who used her to create a scandal in an attempt to destroy your political career."

Archer looked at the papers in his hand again, studying them carefully.

"You say you love my daughter," he said after a long moment.

"Very much, sir."

"You still a hell-raiser like you used to be?"

"I've mellowed with age," Durango replied, and notched his chin upward, "but I still march to the tune of my own drum."

"Good," Judge Archer said. "Abby needs that."

"Excuse me?"

"I've misjudged you, Creed. And I underestimated my daughter. She's got her mother's adventurous nature yes, but she's got a mind all her own and she's learning how to use it well. I guess you're to thank for that."

Durango blinked in surprise. He'd expected animosity from the judge, not an apology.

"I should never have put you in jail for spray-painting your stepmother's warehouse. It was wrong of your father to ask me to do it, but I was wrong not to understand the damage it caused you."

"That means a lot to me, sir, to hear you say that," he said.

"When was the last time you saw your father?" Judge Archer asked.

"Ten years ago. When I left Silverton Heights for good."

"Go see him. I think he just might be in the mood to mend fences."

"Yes, sir. Thank you for the advice." Durango got to his feet.

"Oh." The judge waved a hand. "One more thing."

"Yes?"

"Marry my daughter before you dangle her off any more bridges, will you?"

AFRAID TO DO anything in case it was the wrong move, Abby stayed in bed at the Tranquility Spa. She watched old movies, cried for no reason, tried her best not to think of Durango and waited for a sign.

Cassandra called to check on her. They had a nice conversation and Abby felt closer to her mother than she ever had, but she still hadn't returned her father's calls. She was much too ashamed.

Two days after the awful photograph ran in the

Confidential Inquisitor Abby was propped up in bed watching the noon news when they broke into the program with a special press conference. Judge Archer was going to make an official statement concerning his daughter and the incident that was becoming known to the media as the Satan's Bridge scandal.

Abby watched while her father announced that he was firing his campaign manager Ken Rockford and that he had changed his get-tough policy on juvenile offenders because he had come to realize the drawbacks and limitations to such a rigid stance.

Then he looked straight into the camera. "Abby, sweetheart," he said. "I understand. All is forgiven. I love you. No matter what happens. Please come home."

It was all the sign she needed.

Abby's heart swelled with love for her father. She still belonged. She could go home. Eagerly she packed her bags, bade goodbye to Tess and Jackson, who were cuddling and cooing like lovebirds and practically ran all the way back to Silverton Heights.

"DAD?" Durango pushed through the backyard gate to find his father sitting on the deck staring forlornly at the empty pool.

Slowly Phillip Creed craned his neck to look at his only son.

"Durango?" he said, staring hard as if he were seeing a mirage. "Is that you?"

He hadn't expected it to be so easy to walk right into his father's embrace, but it was. Neither had he expected the rush of emotions to be so high.

Anxiety, sadness, longing but most important, forgiveness.

His dad leaped up from his patio chair, spread out his arms and hugged Durango tight. "My God, you look wonderful."

He patted his dad's shoulders and then stepped back. He wished he could say the same for his father. A decade had passed since Durango had last seen him, but by the worry lines on Phillip's weary face, he appeared twenty years older.

"Sit down, sit down." Phillip waved at a chair. "I was just having breakfast."

Durango looked down at the glass of tomato juice and the Blood Mary mix on the patio table. His dad was drinking on Wednesday morning when he had to be at the office in less than an hour?

Not a good sign.

Glancing around, he noticed other portentous signals. The deck was sagging, the hot tub needed restaining and Durango couldn't remember a time when the pool hadn't been clean and filled with water. The glass tabletop was cloudy, the lawn chairs flecking paint and the cushions were faded and frayed. Rusted scrap metal and other debris were piled in the corner of the lot. It looked as if it had been there for a while.

The once luxurious backyard had gone to ruin.

His father was watching him survey the place. "It's a mess, I know. I've let things get a little run-down."

"What's happened?"

Philip paused, sighed, took a long drink of his Bloody Mary and said, "Meredith left me."

Durango leaned toward the man. "I'm sorry, I didn't know."

"No reason to be sorry." He snorted. "You were right about her all along."

"I don't take comfort in that fact."

"You have a right to gloat. Go ahead. She cleaned me out, son. Not only did she take a huge chunk of my money in the divorce settlement, but her dirty business dealings landed me in legal hot water. By the time I get through with lawyer fees, there won't be much of this to pass on to you." He waved a hand at the house.

Durango cracked a slight smile. "You're undis-owning me?"

"I never disowned you. Never even changed my will even though Meredith was driving me insane to do it. I made a bad mistake, son. I was hurting so badly after your mother died I couldn't see Meredith for the shark she was. I stayed with her because I was too proud to admit I was wrong."

"We all make mistakes."

"I made a doozy. And I don't expect you to forgive me so easily. I hurt you badly."

"There's just one thing that still bothers me," he ventured.

"What's that?"

"How could you have believed that I would try to force myself on Meredith?"

"She was young and sexy and I was jealous. I saw the way she looked at you. I was afraid you wanted her in the same way." Philip made a derisive noise. "Can you believe it? Jealous of my own son."

"Water under the bridge, Dad. I'm back and I forgive you. I hope you'll forgive me."

"There's nothing to forgive you for, son. You did nothing wrong."

"I let my stubbornness and my hurt feelings keep me from coming back to see you. I let my resentment toward you and Meredith and Judge Archer and even the whole of Silverton Heights color my entire outlook."

"Would you consider coming back home, Durango? And helping me straighten out the business, before I lose it, too?"

"Nothing would please me more."

"Thank you."

They hugged again.

"But first we need to get rid of this." Durango reached over for the Bloody Mary and emptied the glass into the dirt.

"You're right. I'm so glad you're here."

"Me, too."

Were those tears in his father's eyes? Durango felt a tightness in his throat and in his heart.

Happiness filled him. He and his father had bridged the gap. They could start fresh, build a new, stronger relationship than the one they'd had even before Durango's mother had died. He was so glad he'd taken the chance and come home.

And this change in him would never have been possible if it weren't for Abby. She had shown him that he was already enough. He didn't have to do or be anything more than he already was in order to earn love. Without even knowing it, she had taught him how to forgive.

Now all he had to do was get her to forgive him.

14

THE BARBECUE HOEDOWN fund-raiser Abby had organized at a local ranch for her father's campaign was going smoothly. The caterers had arrived on time with the correct food. The guests were enjoying the variety of activities from swimming to horseback riding to lounging under tent awnings cooled by fans.

And best of all, the news media was on its best behavior.

In fact, the topic of the day centered on Mack Woodruff and his dirty politics. The judge's approval rating had jumped ten points in the polls. Polls showed that Abby's scandal had turned into a human-interest story and given her father a more approachable appearance. Turns out voters could appreciate a politician openly admitting when he faced challenges with his children, just like everyone else.

Two weeks had passed since she'd come home. Her dad had not only welcomed her back with open arms, but had given her Ken's old job as his campaign manager. He asked her to forgive him for being over-protective and she asked him to forgive her for embarrassing him. And they discovered that the riff between them had in the end strengthened their relationship.

Her father respected her in a way he never had before and she had learned to separate his wants and opinions from her own. They even argued politics now, which they never had before. Abby found the changes liberating.

They never spoke about Durango, but Abby couldn't stop thinking about him. She still felt a combination of emotions. Love, desire, anger, despair.

She had come to realize that even though she'd gotten hurt during the course of their short-lived romance, it had been worth all the pain because she finally felt fully alive.

Durango had given her the gift of her own passion and, for that, she would be forever grateful.

But not a day went by that she didn't look up in the sky, remembering.

"You're doing a great job, sweetheart," her father said, coming over to where Abby was supervising preparations for the barn dance later that evening. "Harry Cornwell just pledged a quarter of a million and he credited you with charming him out of it."

"That's wonderful, Dad."

"Oh," he said. "Did I happen to mention that I hired a stunt pilot to put on a little aerial acrobatic show for the guests?"

"No. Way to keep your campaign manager in-

formed,'' she chided gently. ''I could have arranged
to have bleachers brought in.''

''I took care of that.'' As he spoke a large truck
bearing a section of bleachers rumbled into the driveway of the ranch.

Her father checked his watch. ''The plane should
be here in twenty minutes.

A crew set up the bleachers. The guests took their
seats. Abby was busy chatting up supporters when the
hum of a biplane engine drew everyone's attention.

For ten minutes, the plane swooped and dove and
did acrobatics. Abby's heart soared along with the
plane. She wished she was in the sky, winging on air.

And then the plane began skywriting.

The sight of the white smoke brought back a poke
of sharp memories as she recalled that day on the
mesa when she'd seen the plane write ''Freefall''
above the red rock bluffs of Sedona.

The crowd spelled out the letters as the plane
looped out the writing.

A. B. B. Y.

It took a minute for her to realize it was her name
being spelled across the sky. She put a hand to her
heart and was surprised to discover it was beating
erratically.

A. R. C. H. E. R.

All eyes turned to stare at Abby.

What was up? It wasn't her birthday or anything
special.

W. I. L. L.

She shot a glance at her father. "What gives?"

He grinned wide. "Keep watching."

Y. O. U.

She felt her throat close off. Tears filled her eyes. Her stomach squeezed in anticipation of the next word.

"M." shouted the crowd.

"A."

"R."

By the time the pilot got to the second *R* in marry, Abby's knees buckled and she sat down hard on the ground.

"You okay, darling?" Her father was at her side. She fumbled for his hand. He squeezed it.

"Durango?" she whispered.

"Who else?"

"But...but, you were in on this together?"

Her father nodded. "It's going to be okay. Take a deep breath."

"You approve of him?"

"You both have my blessings."

After the pilot spelled out M.E., he climbed higher into the sky and a man dropped out in a parachute.

Two minutes later, Durango was on the ground, unclipping himself from the parachute. Once he was untangled, Abby flung herself into his arms.

Here he was at last. Her soul mate, her life partner,

the man she loved with every fiber of her being. The man she had always loved.

His black eyes snapped with passion and his sexy lips were curled in a wicked grin. Her heart stuttered and she forgot to breathe.

Their gazes coupled, locked.

The warmth of his daredevil eyes filled her up. It was a look so hot and weighted with such meaning she felt as if he'd actually reached out and touched her in a spot so secret she hadn't known it existed.

"Well," he said. "So what do you say? Can you forgive me enough to marry me?"

Abby looked around and realized the crowd was holding its collective breath, waiting for her answer.

"Yes," she whispered with all the passion she had in her. "Yes, yes, yes."

The crowd burst into wild applause.

He kissed her as he'd never kissed her before. He kissed her as if the very fate of the world depended on her.

When he finished, they looked up to see her father smiling his approval and dangling a key on his fingers. "Feel free to use my trailer," he said. "It's parked at the back of the campground."

Abby blushed, but did not sneeze and accepted the key. "Thank you, Daddy."

Her father kissed her cheek. "Thank you, darling, for teaching this old dog a few new tricks. Now go on. You two go talk things through. I can handle the fund-raiser from here on out.''

Abby sprinted ahead of Durango, making him chase her.

Before the door even closed behind them, Durango had her in his arms, kissing her again.

Abby shut her eyes and dissolved into him. Hugging him around the neck, she mewled softly in his ear.

He was her fire, she thought dreamily. Her flame. With Durango beside her, she could never lose touch with the passion that burned deep inside her.

His fingers deftly unbuttoned her blouse and it seemed to magically fall away. He inched a hand up underneath her bra to unhook it.

Her breasts engorged and her nipples flowered at his touch. She opened her eyes and looked into his face to convince herself this wasn't a dream, that Durango had actually asked her to marry him.

''I'm not a dream, Angel. This is happening for real,'' he said, reading her mind.

''Why did you wait two whole weeks to come to me?'' She playfully swatted his arm. ''You deserve to be punished for torturing me like that.''

''It was torture for me, too, but your dad thought it would be much more romantic for me to ask you this way even if it meant I had to wait two weeks for the right occasion.''

"It was pretty spectacular," she said. "It'll make a great tale for the grandkids."

"No second-rate proposal for my passionate lady," he said.

"So, it appears that you've mended fences with my father."

"And mine."

"That's so wonderful. You've forgiven everyone who wronged you?"

"And they've forgiven me. All that's left is you. Can you possibly forgive me for treating you so shabbily?"

"Of course I've forgiven you. Besides I was the one who wanted nothing more than a red-hot fling. Remember?"

"I guess I sort of put a crimp in those plans," he teased.

"Hey, babe, crimp away. The only reason I wanted that red-hot fling is because even after ten years I couldn't stop having midnight fantasies about you. I thought I could sex you out of my system, but I was wrong. Turns out I'm hooked and there's nothing I can do about it."

"Just my luck," he murmured, still studiously kissing her eyelids, her nose, her cheeks.

"So where are we going to live? Here or Sedona?"

"I'm helping my dad get back on his feet so it'll work out best all the way around if we stay in Phoenix," he replied, "but I'm not giving up my place in

Sedona. So we can have a getaway spot anytime we're in the mood for vortex sex.''

"Did I ever tell you, I like the way you think?''

"Not nearly often enough.''

Her heart thumped beneath his hand. He buried his mouth against her neck and her pulse fluttered from the searing heat of his naughty tongue.

He smelled of man and rich red Arizona soil, and his skin was toasty warm beneath her fingers.

Her blood streamed feverishly hot through her veins. She wanted him so badly she couldn't stand herself. She wriggled her slacks past her hips and viciously kicked them off.

Then she took his big masculine hand and guided him where she wanted him to go. When he found her slick, ready wetness, she hissed in her breath and bit down softly on his bottom lip.

"Make love to me, Durango. Two weeks without you is too long.''

He lifted her into his arms and carried her to the bed. She felt as if she had at last roused from an infinite slumber to discover her real life had finally began.

Swiftly, wordlessly he tossed off his flight suit and then the clothes underneath. He kicked off his underwear and she shimmied out of her panties.

Once naked, he tugged her bottom to the edge of the mattress while he stood on the floor. He separated her thighs and greedily plunged into her, groaning as her slick heat encased him.

They'd been apart too long for foreplay.

Abby hissed in her breath at the swiftness of their impact. They were both so desperately hungry. Arching her back, she raised her hips up to welcome his eager thrusts, urging him on.

"Yes, yes," she cried.

This was what she had been longing for, what had been missing. This vibrating connection, this electromagnetic force far greater than either him or her. This vast, wonderful, forgiving love.

The vigor of their union raided her mind of rational thought. She could do nothing but travel the ripple of scrumptious delight, urging him on by clamping her legs around his hips and pulling him deeper inside her.

More. More. She had to have more.

He matched her frantic thrashing and she knew this first time would be fast and frenzied. Durango tried to control himself. Abby saw the tussle screw up his features as he battled to slow their lovemaking.

"Let go," she whispered, and he gave up the struggle. With a feeble moan, he dropped into ecstasy.

His reckless sounds, his headlong thrust exploded into her own climax.

Shuddering wave after shuddering wave rippled through her body, lifting her up to glorious peaks. A keening wail ripped its way up through her throat and mingled with Durango's harsh noise. Their sounds reverberated sexily around the small space.

He collapsed onto the bed beside her, wrapped his arms around her and brought her along with him. After flipping Durango onto his back, Abby rested astride his waist.

She sprawled against his chest and he tightened his arms around her.

"I love you, Abby." He breathed, a heady catch in his voice.

She pressed her lips to the hollow of his throat. "I love you too, Durango," she whispered.

They stayed locked together for a long time. Abby realized she'd never felt so complete, so content, so whole.

Love for her shone in his eyes, and in Durango's eyes she saw her own passion flow. He loved her for who she really was deep inside.

She kissed him. Slow, soft and languid. There wasn't any hurry. They had the rest of their lives.

Epilogue

"YOU KNOW WHAT you need?"

"What?"

"Something blue." Tess held up a lacy blue hanky. "I've got two."

"Haven't you heard? I don't need a hanky. I don't sneeze anymore."

"Not since you learned to embrace your passion and stop denying your true self."

Abby stared at her best friend who looked resplendent in her wedding dress, Abby thought the same about her own.

In the church, the guests waited as did their anxious grooms.

Six months ago, when they first arrived in Sedona, neither one of them knew—that discovering the power of the vortex was an event that would change their lives forever.

The pianist played "The Wedding March."

"I guess we're up," Tess said, as they hugged each other.

Then together, they turned and walked down the aisle on the arms of their fathers.

A double wedding. Two best friends had found their true loves at the very same time. Abby's heart filled to overflowing.

The governor-elect squeezed her hand. "I'm so proud of you," her father said. "And of Durango."

"Thanks, Daddy, that means a lot."

Cassandra and her young boy toy waved to them as they walked past. Her mother was unique, a one-of-a-kind character. Abby was glad for the Gypsy blood that kept her excited, but just as appreciative of her father's steady, calming influence. She had the best of both worlds.

Cassandra winked and mouthed, *You gotta have passion.*

Abby looked down the length of the aisle and caught Durango's gaze. Oh, she had passion. In spades.

Then she was standing beside Durango. A smile lit up his face. "You're so beautiful," he whispered reverently.

He squeezed her hand while the minister married Tess and Jackson. *I'm here,* that squeeze told her. *Now and forever.*

Abby's heart hitched, her gaze fixed on the strong-willed, adventuresome man who had helped her define the person she had yearned to become.

The well-rounded person she was whenever she looked into his loving eyes. They complemented one another, each bringing something vital to the relationship. Together, they had found the perfect balance.

After the minister pronounced them husband and wife, Durango swept her into his arms and kissed her with a heated fever she had come to joyfully anticipate.

This was what she'd been craving all those years. Closeness, intimacy, love.

As Durango held her close and the crowd applauded, Abby pressed her lips to his ear and whispered, "Let's slip off someplace private before the reception."

"Angel." He chuckled. "What are you suggesting?"

"You know." She felt her face blush hot.

"Come on." He winked. "If you want it, you've got to ask for it."

"All right, Durango Creed, drag me off and make wild passionate love to me because I want you to and well, I've just gotta have it."